CODA

TED STAUNTON

CODA

ORCA BOOK PUBLISHERS

Library and Archives Canada Cataloguing in Publication

Staunton, Ted, 1956-, author
Coda / Ted Staunton.
(The seven sequels)

Issued in print and electronic formats.
ISBN 978-1-4598-0549-1 (pbk.).--ISBN 978-1-4598-0550-7 (pdf).--
ISBN 978-1-4598-0551-4 (epub)

I. Title.
PS8587.T334C63 2014   jc813'.54   C2014-901551-8
C2014-901552-6

First published in the United States, 2014
Library of Congress Control Number: 2014935390

Summary: When Spencer's brother, Bunny, is kidnapped in Toronto, Spencer is
forced to deal with fallout from their grandfather's murky past.

*Orca Book Publishers is dedicated to preserving the environment and has
printed this book on Forest Stewardship Council® certified paper.*

Orca Book Publishers gratefully acknowledges the support for its publishing
programs provided by the following agencies: the Government of Canada
through the Canada Book Fund and the Canada Council for the Arts,
and the Province of British Columbia through the BC Arts Council
and the Book Publishing Tax Credit.

Design by Chantal Gabriell
Cover photography by Corbis Images, Dreamstime, CG Textures and iStock

ORCA BOOK PUBLISHERS
PO Box 5626, Stn. B
Victoria, BC Canada
V8R 6S4

ORCA BOOK PUBLISHERS
PO Box 468
Custer, WA USA
98240-0468

www.orcabook.com
Printed and bound in Canada.

17 16 15 14 • 4 3 2 1

To Seven kith and kin:
Eric, John, Norah, Richard, Shane and Sigmund

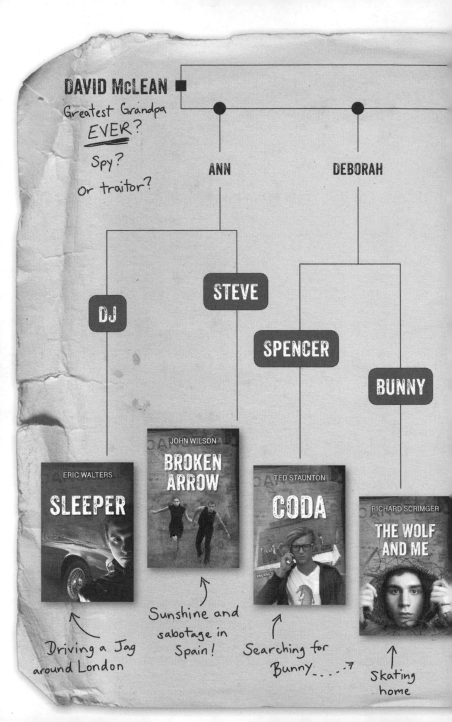

DAVID McLEAN ■

Greatest Grandpa
 <u>EVER</u>?

 Spy?

 Or traitor?

ANN

DEBORAH

DJ

STEVE

SPENCER

BUNNY

ERIC WALTERS

SLEEPER

JOHN WILSON

BROKEN ARROW

TED STAUNTON

CODA

RICHARD SCRIMGER

THE WOLF AND ME

← Driving a Jag around London

↑ Sunshine and sabotage in Spain!

↑ Searching for Bunny.....

↑ Skating home

MELANIE COLE

VERA McLEAN

CHARLOTTE   VICTORIA   SUZANNE

ADAM

WEBB

RENNIE

SIGMUND BROUWER
TIN SOLDIER

SHANE PEACOCK
DOUBLE YOU

NORAH McCLINTOCK
FROM THE DEAD

On the road in
the Deep South

Channeling
James Bond

Nazi-hunting
in Detroit

READ THE ORIGINAL
SEVEN (THE SERIES)

www.seventheseries.com

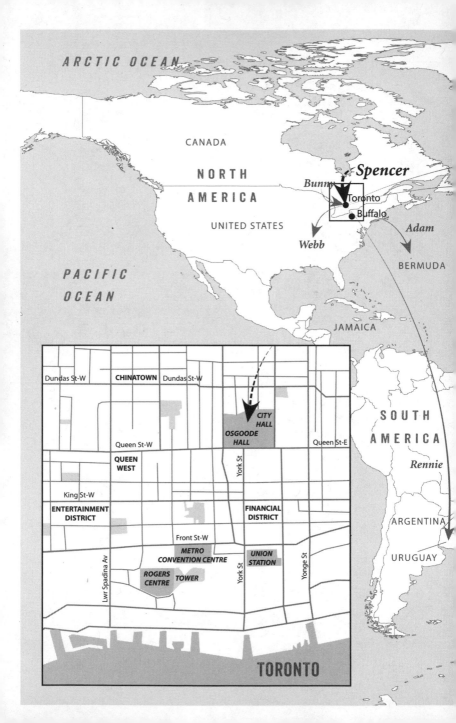

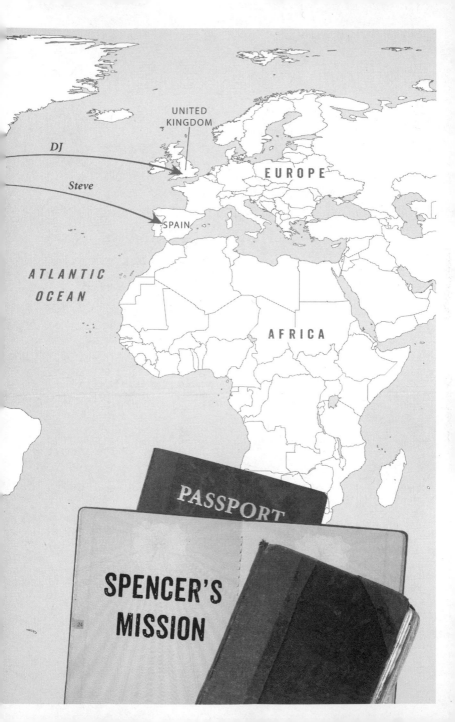

coda n. *final passage of piece of music, usu. elaborate or distinct*
—POCKET OXFORD ENGLISH DICTIONARY

"What are you, English, a paid assassin, a hired killer?"
"All soldiers are that," I said.
—LEN DEIGHTON, *BILLION-DOLLAR BRAIN*

ONE

Bunny's gone. I stepped off the ice to get us sausages from the truck, which *he* wanted (my brother doesn't get street meat these days), and now, when I turn back, he's vanished.

What's with that? I hoover a sausage and scope the place. I saw the latest James Bond movie before Christmas, and I've been doing his laser stare ever since. I think I rock it, even with glasses. Q should be talking in my earbud.

The rink at city hall is hopping tonight: skaters in bright colors, Christmas decorations, tinny music, cold.

At the far side, the scaffolding is set up for the New Year's Eve concert stage. This year it's Aiden Tween. Since I'm not a twelve-year-old girl, I plan to miss it. Meanwhile, the hiss of blades on ice reminds me of the Komodo dragons Bond escaped from in *Skyfall.* I whip out my phone and grab a few seconds of video. I imagine an overhead shot, patterns of people flowing, Bond zipping through them. Hey, a chase scene on ice! I bet no one's ever done it. I could use Bunny—he's a good skater.

But Bunny's not skating. Maybe he's hit the washroom. Before I check, I take time to polish off his sausage too. I guess I'm hungrier than I thought. Besides, Bunny's not the only person I'm looking for. I haven't seen AmberLea since September, and it might be nice to meet her on my own.

I don't see AmberLea either. I fire Bun a text— where r u—then AmberLea: skating remember? I turn to look for Bunny near the sausage truck and hear my ringtone, those eerie first notes from *The Good, the Bad and the Ugly.* I dig out my phone again. AmberLea has texted: pan 180. I get it; AmberLea is in first-year film school, like me. I turn around and there she is, on the ice right behind me.

"Hey!" I say.

"Spencer!" It's not Oscar-quality dialogue, but I'll take it. AmberLea's arms are stretched out. Is this for a hello hug or just for balance? Should I go for the hug? What if it's a bad call? I solve the problem by forgetting I'm wearing skates as I step forward. I stumble onto the ice and practically land on top of her.

"Whoa!" She helps me stand up. "Hey, new glasses. Like 'em."

I fumble them back into place. I've replaced my wire frames with clunky black ones, which are very cool right now. Plus, they go with the old curling sweater I found in a vintage store, decorated with crossed brooms and deer antlers. I am now urban cool. AmberLea says, "There's mustard on your chin."

"What? Oh, sorry." I swipe at my chin. So much for cool.

"No problem." She gives me a real hug. AmberLea looks great, as usual. Her blond hair sweeps out from under the same kind of hat Dad got Bunny and me for Christmas. I instantly revise my opinion on wooly yellow-and-blue hats with earflaps and tie strings. Maybe I'll wear mine after all. I see she has matching mittens too. All in all, AmberLea makes a great picture—until someone else barges into the frame. A big guy showers me with ice flakes in a perfect hockey stop. "This is Toby," AmberLea says. "We're friends at school."

"Hey," says Toby. He's wearing the same hat. I re-revise my opinion and make a mental note to give my hat to the first street person I see. Underneath the hat, Toby has a perfect swoop of brown hair and a perfect, stubbly face above a perfect suede bomber jacket with a perfect long, preppy scarf that matches the hat. I know his skates are expensive, because Bunny has the same kind. I hate him already.

I shake hands with Toby (who does *that*?), trying for my best manly man grip. He says, "AmberLea's told me about you," in some kind of clipped American accent. I wonder which parts she told him.

"She was probably just kidding," I say.

Toby laughs. That doesn't help.

"So," AmberLea says, "let's skate." Uh-oh. I was so anxious to see AmberLea, I never thought about the actual skating part. The only ice I can handle is in a glass of Scotch—and that's not even my line; it's from a movie about a killer glacier. I don't even drink Scotch.

"Um," I say, "actually, I have to look for Bunny."

They both look surprised. How much has AmberLea told this guy? "Bunny?" AmberLea says. "Isn't he…?"

I nod. "But he's home for Christmas. It's complicated. He was with me and now he's gone, and he's only supposed to be with family, so I have to find him."

"Can we help?" Toby asks.

"Naw, it's okay. You skate. He's probably just in the washroom. When I find him, we'll come back." Or maybe not. Maybe I'll just go somewhere and die.

"Where are the washrooms?" says AmberLea.

"Over there." I point to the far end of the rink.

"C'mon, we'll skate over with you."

"Oh, that's okay."

"*C'mon.*" AmberLea beckons and does a nifty little backup glide.

Oh, man. What can I do? "Bloody hell," I whisper in my best Brit accent. *Man up, Bond.* Right. Notice James Bond never skates? I push off carefully. Except for falling over, wobbling forward is all I can do on skates. I keep my hands out, legs spread wide enough to drive the sausage truck between them. I'm swearing in a steady stream under my breath.

This is Bun's fault. He's the one who wanted to skate. He'd even wanted to skate on the lake up at Grandpa's cottage yesterday if the ice was strong enough. Then all the crazy stuff happened, and we forgot about it. As soon as we got home today, Bunny said, "Come on, Spence. My only chance, maybe."

I was good with it. AmberLea and her mom were in town, staying at the hotel across the street from city hall. I texted her, figuring we'd sit on a bench and talk while Bun skated. I really wanted to tell her about what had happened at the cottage. Besides, I felt kind of sorry for Bun. He's not exactly having fun these days.

Now I'm not having fun, and AmberLea and Toby are politely pretending not to notice. Toby is skating backward, which does not make me like him any better. My exit is coming up. If I glide now, I should run out of gas as my toes bump the end of the rink. This is good, because I don't know how to stop either.

AmberLea and Toby start their turn. I don't. "Back in a bit," I call. AmberLea waves. My toes kiss the edge of the rink.

TWO

Bond hopped out of the Komodo-dragon pit like a kid vaulting a backyard fence. I stagger off the ice like the Creature climbing out of the Black Lagoon. My fingers are cold, my feet are hurting, and AmberLea is with a preppy skating hunk. Still, things could be worse: I could have fallen over, for example. Or Roz could be calling. I wouldn't want to tell her the Bun-man's not available.

Which means it's time to find the guy. I clomp across the rubber mats to the washroom. Bunny's not there. I do a quick foot check under stall doors to be sure. I feel dumb doing this, but it's slightly better than calling "Bunny?" in a men's room. Bond could dice anybody who laughed at him into a small bowl of mush—so could Bunny, for that matter. I don't even dice carrots.

I clomp back to the rink. No Bunny. Now I'm confused and a little bugged.

"Find him?" AmberLea pulls up. I shake my head. My ringtone sounds. "*The Good, the Bad,*" says AmberLea. "Nice." Apart from the fact that she's saved my life twice, this is another reason why I think AmberLea and I are perfect for each other.

I check my phone. It's a text from Bunny: donut call cops. "Oh, great." I show it to AmberLea as Toby skates up.

"Whaaat?" she says. "He's on a donut run with some cops?"

I shake my head. "Naw, he's a bad speller. He means 'do not.' My guess is, he met some of his buds from last summer and went with them. Now he's remembered he can't do that, and he's scared I'll call Roz."

"Roz?"

"I'll tell you later. Listen," I say, "I better go, in case he heads home."

"Really?" AmberLea has this way of tucking her chin into her neck when she's doubtful. Does that mean she doesn't want me to go?

"That's too bad," says Toby. Yeah right, I think.

"Okay," says AmberLea. "Plan B: tomorrow afternoon, you have to come with us. Remember I messaged you that we sold my grandma's cottage?"

"Yeah," I say. "And speaking of cottages, wait till I tell you about—"

"No!" says AmberLea. "I have to tell you about Grandma's first. Guess who bought it? Aiden Tween! He bought the whole south side of the lake. And he's a big fan of Grandma's movies, so he wants to meet me, and he said I could bring friends."

"Really?" I'm stunned. Like I said, Aiden Tween is not my thing. His tweenybopper music is either bubblegum ballads or techno dance crud (remember his Comet Shuffle dance move?), but it's not like I hang with megastars on a daily basis. Maybe I could shoot some video, post it, the whole deal. Jump-start my career. *Cinema verité*, as my doc prof would say. "Wow," I say. "Can Bun come too?"

"Sure," says AmberLea. "I'll text you." She gives me a wave. Toby slips his arm through hers and off they skate.

I find the bench my shoes are under. Unlacing my skates gives me the best feeling I've had since I found out Christmas break is nearly a month long when you're in college. Then I reach for my sneakers and discover something weird: Bunny's sneakers are under here too. Where the heck would he go in his skates? Still, it's typical Bunny. My brother is kind of a special guy. I gather all our stuff and head for O'Toole Central, trying not to think about Toby and AmberLea.

When I get home, the door is unlocked and the house is a disaster—way messier than we left it. If this were a movie, I'd say the place had been searched. In real life, I'd say Bunny and his friends dropped by to get shoes and a snack for three hundred. I stuff the scattered sheet music back in the piano bench, take it off the couch, stick shades back on lamps and put things back in the fridge. The rest I'll deal with later. I'm not going to call Mom unless Roz calls before he gets back. Then it'll hit the fan. *Donut call the cops.* Thanks, Bun; I won't. I'll just wait for Roz to call and melt the phone line. In the meantime, I'll do what I always do when things are a little tense: watch some movies. I think I'll start with *Blade Runner*.

THREE

Probably I should tell you some things in case this gets any weirder. Most of it has to do with my grandpa, David McLean. Grandpa D (my mom's dad) died last June, and in his will, he asked all his grandsons to do some stuff for him. Because I like movies, he wanted me to track down his favorite old movie actress, Gloria Lorraine, and film her giving me a kiss for him. I did it, but things got a little crazy, what with the bikers and the Buffalo mob and the street posse all chasing the stolen Cadillac. Anyway, that's another story, except it was how I met AmberLea, Gloria Lorraine's granddaughter. AmberLea lives in Buffalo, and she got mixed up in it all too, along with Al and Mister Bones, the chihuahua. That's when she saved my life.

Even if I hadn't met AmberLea, I'd still say I got off easy. Ask my cousin DJ—he had to climb Mount Kilimanjaro. Or Bunny. Especially Bunny. Bunny had to get a tattoo, and he ended up with a street gang called the Fifteenth Street Posse. Now he's in Creekside Juvenile Detention Centre. That's another story too.

Anyway, this fall I started film school. Bunny was in Creekside. Deb, our mom, booked a cruise with her sisters for between Christmas and New Year's. Our dad, Jer, was going to visit his dad, Grandpa Bernie, at the same time. Grandpa Bernie lives out west, on Salt Spring Island. They planned to spend a few days chilling in a yurt, getting in touch with their toes or something. Jer invited me to come along, but compare that to a week of parent-free living and you can probably see why I said no thanks.

But that's where Grandpa D comes back in. In November, around when Deb and Jer booked their trips, one of my profs showed my class a rough cut of a documentary he's working on, about this weird country called Pianvia. And I do mean weird: stuff like cards and unicycles has been banned there since 1952 or something. Music too. Don't ask me why. Now the Save Pianvia Counterrevolutionary Army was fighting back, planning an invasion and streaming in classic rock and Texas Hold 'em online, except that no one in Pianvia has a computer. It was complicated. Anyway, I had downloaded the doc onto my laptop and had it with me one time on a visit to Bun. Deb and Jer were busy having some kind of Official Meeting, so I showed Bun some of it, just for laughs. We got to this part about how Zoltan Blum, Pianvia's greatest composer, defected in the 1950s and then later on got murdered. Up came a picture of a mystery man thought to be his killer and Bunny said, "Hey, that's Grandpa!"

"Right, Bun. Get a grip."

"It is. It's an old Grandpa."

Actually, it would have had to be a *young* Grandpa, but I knew what Bun meant. I clicked back. "Grandpa didn't have a mustache, glasses and blond hair, Bun."

"His hair was white. Same as."

"Come on, Bun-man. That's because he was old."

Bun made me email my prof right then, telling him that the mystery guy could maybe be David McLean.

My prof thanked me, but he said the Blum murder was just a sidelight to the larger story and he didn't want to give it more screen time, especially if the ID was just a guess. I thought Bun was wrong anyway, so I forgot all about it.

Meanwhile, some of my cousins and I planned to stay at Grandpa's cottage over the Christmas break. Then we found out Bunny could come home for ten days on the Constructive Rebound for Adolescents Program. Not only was this good news, but it also made for a great acronym. Deb and Jer couldn't change their flights. Cousin DJ said he'd "look after" us (sometimes DJ thinks he's Grandpa), and when I heard AmberLea and her mom were coming to town, I hoped DJ might cover Bunny for me if I came back down to the city. He's family, after all.

When Bunny got home a few days before Christmas, I was watching the doc again for an assignment. "Hey," Bun said, "the Grandpa movie!" and we got into it all over again. Finally, I took my laptop into the kitchen. Jer was baking Christmas shortbread. "What color was Grandpa David's hair before it went white?" I asked.

Jer shrugged. "Dark. He was already pretty gray when I met him."

Deb came up from her office in the basement, carrying some exams she'd been marking. She's a philosophy prof at York U. "What color was your dad's hair?" Jer asked, brushing flour off his flannel shirt.

"And did he ever have a mustache?" I put in.

"Brown," Deb said. "No mustache. He said he tried one in the war but it was a disaster. Why?"

I showed her the photo on the screen. "Bun thinks that's Grandpa."

Deb put on her glasses and peered. "Well, there's a vague resemblance, but…" She shrugged. "Who is it?"

"Some mystery killer in the 60s," I say. "In Pianvia. Europe, I mean. He killed a Pianvian guy who defected."

Deb did a classic double take. Then she laughed. "Dream on, guys. Apart from the war, the closest Grandpa got to a killing was a good business deal."

"Except for the ants," Bun said.

"Right," said Deb. "Remember I told you how he cornered the market on—"

"Souvenir snow globes for the '72 Canada–Russia hockey series," Jer finished for her. He pushed his bandanna higher up his forehead. Now he had flour all over it too.

Deb frowned. "Souvenir *pucks*, actually."

"Right. And then there were the Chinese golf balls or whatever."

"Ping-Pong balls. The golf balls were Cuban."

"What about the wooden Frisbees?"

"Australian. Kind of like boomerangs. Okay, some were mistakes. But don't knock it, buster. My dad built a solid import/export business and gave us a good life."

"I'm not knocking anything," Jer said. Actually, he was knocking butter and sugar and flour around in a bowl. "He did get around though. Maybe he was a *secret agent.*"

Deb laughed and swatted him with the exams. "Your grasp of logic and evidence is right up there with my students." Then she wiped flour off the exam papers.

And that was that, until our folks went away and we drove up to the cottage with DJ. Bun took his skates. I took the movie on my phone, because Bun wanted me to show the picture to everyone.

We got there first. Bun went outside to chop wood. DJ was at the door, giving orders and calling out to Adam and Webb, who'd just pulled in. I was laying a fire with the scraps of wood left inside from the fall. I grabbed the last piece, which was leaning up against the paneling by the fireplace. It stuck, which was weird. I yanked hard. It gave, and I tumbled backward with the wood and a square of paneling attached to it. A jumble of things spilled out from behind the panel, including a Walther PPK, James Bond's weapon of choice.

FOUR

Everybody helped lay the stuff out on the kitchen table. There was money from all over the world, a net bag of golf balls with Russian printing, a cheesy wig and beard, passports from different countries with different names but all with Grandpa's picture, a notebook and an envelope. On the front of the envelope you could read the imprint of some words: *You are a traitor. You deserve to die.*

You can see why everyone got a little crazy. DJ went ballistic when he saw the *traitor* note. In ten seconds flat, we'd all decided Grandpa was a spy. Then I wasn't so sure. Grandpa D was more than a bit of a practical joker. He'd flip the plane upside down if you were flying with him, that kind of thing. In fact, for a while last summer I'd thought the adventure with Gloria Lorraine was a trick he'd set up too.

This was too perfect. DJ was paging through the notebook, saying, "The words don't make sense," and I said, "Maybe it's *secret code*," remembering the way Jer had teased Deb back at home.

"I think you're right," DJ said. He's not wired for sarcasm. It didn't matter, because that's when the gun went off. That flipped *all* of us out.

"What do we do now?" Webb asked when things calmed down.

Bun made the only intelligent suggestion. "Maybe we should call our moms." It was too late. DJ was already yelling and tearing apart the notebook, matching parts of it up with the passports.

"Okay, so they connect," Webb said, still reasonable. "Now what?"

"Nothing," Adam said. "Unless we're going to all these places to figure it all out."

Right, I thought. You go, boys.

I chipped in with, "Yeah! We have, like, whole *hours* before our parents would know we were gone!"

Turns out none of them were wired for sarcasm. Next thing you know, everyone was grabbing money and passports and notebook pages. I think Adam had a flight booked before I could open the potato chips.

Bun and I, naturally, weren't going anywhere. Bun would have had a little trouble with borders, for one thing, and I was going to meet up with AmberLea.

"But the movie picture," Bun said. "See? It fits. There's a disguise kit."

"That disguise stuff wouldn't fool a four-year-old," I said. "And his hair's the wrong color. All those passports had photos of Grandpa the way he really looked. Plus, there was nothing about Pianvia. Anyway, they think he's a spy, not a hit man. We'll tell Mom about this stuff, like you said. That was a good idea. I bet it's all junk from some spy-theme party Grandpa threw a million years ago."

"What about the gun?"

"Maybe Grandpa got it when he flew bush planes in Africa. I dunno, Bun."

And I really didn't. When DJ dropped us off in Toronto, I said, "Guess you can't hang with Bun this aft, huh?"

He gave me a get-real look. "I've got to scan and email this stuff to Steve in Spain. Then I've got a flight to London, Spence."

"Right."

His window hummed shut. We waved as he drove away. "Let's go skating," Bunny said.

FIVE

DECEMBER 28

I wake up to a blank laptop screen and the bleat of our landline. I stagger off the couch and find the phone in its cradle in the kitchen. On the way I catch a bleary glimpse of the time on the clock radio: 8:03 AM. Sickeningly early. Ever since classes ended, I'd forgotten this time existed. I'm going to start a religion that bans getting up before noon on holidays. Maybe it would be a good fit for Pianvia. Everything else is banned there.

I hit the Talk button mid-bleat. "Hello?" I sound as if I've been gargling with those Russian golf balls.

"Roz Inbow here. Who am I speaking with, please?" Forget the "please"; the voice has all the cozy charm of a falling anvil. *Roz*. Instantly I'm awake, remembering last night. Unfortunately, I'm not awake enough to keep from blurting, "Spencer."

"Bernard's brother. Let me speak to Bernard, please."

"Uh, it's awfully early."

"It's way past the time he's used to. Let me speak to him, please."

"Just a sec."

I climb the stairs with the phone on *Mute*. My heart is pounding, but not from the climb. Bun's door is half open. I have no idea what time I dozed off, but I know he wasn't back then. He'd better be here now. I have no clue what I'm going to tell Roz if he isn't.

Roz, if you haven't guessed, is Bun's CRAP release supervisor. She can yank him back to Creekside and add more time to his sentence if he screws up—like by hanging with his street posse or not checking in.

I look in Bun's room: empty. Oh. No. If things were halfway normal around here, I'd be handing this off to Deb or Jer. Scratch that. I wouldn't even be *up*. But things aren't normal. I try the only thing I can think of: I imitate Jer. People tell me I sound like him on the phone. Of course, the last time I pretended to be someone else, it almost got four people and a dog killed. I do a frantic throat-clear—*la-la-la* count to ten—to ditch the Russian golf balls. Then I lift the phone again and try to mellow it out. "Hello?"

"I'm calling for *Bernard*," Roz's voice clangs. "Who am I speaking to, please?"

"This is"—throat clear—"Jerry O'Toole, Bun—*Bernard*'s father. What can I do for you?"

"Roz Inbow here. I need to speak to Bernard. He was due for a ten-PM check-in call last night that he failed to complete."

"Riiiiight. Well, we were having some family time last night, Roz, and I guess we all forgot. My bad. But he's right here, sound asleep. The Monopoly game ran a little late. I'm just up myself. How 'bout I have him call you later?"

There's a pause at the other end. Maybe Roz is swallowing a nail or two. Then I hear a sigh and she says, "By ten o'clock. At the latest. You have the number."

"Cool. Sure do. I'll make sure he calls. Have a good one."

"Uh-huh. Oh, and Mister O'Toole? I thought you were away."

"Just back," I say fast, and I hit the Off button before I get in any deeper.

But I am in deeper, aren't I? Now I've really got to find Bunny. I check my phone for messages. There's one from AmberLea last night—meet hotel lobby @1. Nothing from Bun. I call his cell: no answer. I text, call me NOW then call roz b4 trubl.

I deal with an urgent need to pee and then go back to the kitchen. I put in toast, pour juice and think about my next move. Bun's already messed up my time with AmberLea; she's only here a few days.

Sipping juice, I stare dully at the back-door jumble of shoes and boots. I look a little closer, then go down the hall and look at the front-door jumble. Bunny's skates aren't there. His boots are. All he's got are the boots, which he never wears, and the sneakers I brought back from the rink. He couldn't have come home and left still wearing skates. Could he? Then why was the door unlocked? A prickle runs up my neck. I look around again. Last night's plain old mess turns sinister. Why was Deb's rocker on the dining-room table? Why was sheet music scattered around the room? Did someone break in and search the place? But who? And for what? Nothing seems to be missing—except Bunny and his blades. Which means either he's still wearing them or he got shoes someplace else.

The toaster dings in the kitchen. The only place I can think Bunny might be is where the Fifteenth Street Posse hangs. *Oh, great.* On the other hand, I'm so creeped-out thinking someone might have searched the house that a little outing might be nice. If I can't find Bun, I'll call Deb on her cruise. Jer's cell service is useless on Salt Spring Island.

I crunch down the toast, change my T-shirt (did I really leave my room this messy?), get my curling sweater and grab the keys to the minivan from their hook in the kitchen. Jer said the van was for emergencies only; I'd say this counts. On the way out, I double-check that the door locks behind me. Then I go looking for my brother.

SIX

When I finally get the van started (the O'Toolemobile is not exactly an Aston Martin), I drive west, then south to Lake Shore. It's not far, really. The Fifteenth Street Posse hangs at a gym on guess which street? I drove by it once with Jer when Bun was on trial.

The closer I get, the sketchier things seem: empty storefronts, a Goodwill, a muffler-repair shop, corner variety stores. I turn down Fifteenth Street. There's a Domino's pizza place with a sagging Christmas wreath. Next to it is the gym, a brick box with no doors or windows to the street. It's been tagged all over, including with a striped 15. I pass an alleyway on the far side. A police cruiser is slowly rolling up it. There must be a door down there somewhere. I pull over beside a sign that says SCHOOL CROSSING 30 km. Ahead, the street is lined with matchbox-sized houses, their roof lines as saggy as the Christmas wreath. Then come a couple of low-rise apartment buildings. A few balconies are strung with Christmas lights or stars. Some are still lit. They flap and flicker in the breeze, as if they're about to be blown out. Beyond that is the lake, gray as the pavement and sky.

I don't get out. Maybe it's the neighborhood, or the cops, or just the gritty light, but this feels like every gangster movie I've ever seen. The Posse was one of the gangs chasing AmberLea and me last summer. Even if they liked Bunny, they won't be happy to see me. Oh, man. What would Bond do? Well, he wouldn't wimp out. On the other hand, he's a killing machine with a Walther PPK. I have my glasses and a wooly yellow-and-blue hat with tie strings that I left at home.

Bond might take time out to have a martini and make a plan though. It's too early for martinis, and I've never had one anyway, but I could go back to the Tim Hortons I passed a ways back, have a coffee and make my own plan before I walk down that alley. The police car rolls by. One of the cops gives me a long stare that makes me feel guilty. I swing the van around and head back to Tim's.

Inside Tim's, before my glasses fog up, I see that it's practically dead. I wipe my lenses while I order a triple-triple. I don't like the taste of coffee much, but it's manlier than hot chocolate and a whipped-cream mustache. By the time the girl behind the counter brings it to me, I can see again. I'm glad I can: she's a total babe, even in a hairnet and a frumpy, brown Tim's outfit. I've seen her before: in the visitors' room at Creekside. She was there, wearing a green dress, one day we went to visit Bun. She was holding Bunny's hand when we came in.

"Geez, Bun," I'd said later.

"Yeah, I know." He'd kind of grinned.

"Hey," I blurt out now, "Jade, right?" This could save me a trip to the gym.

"Jane." Her face goes blank and she points to her name tag.

"You know my brother."

She gives me a cold look Roz would probably appreciate. I'm too excited to care. This is the first break I've had. "No," I say, "you do. Bunny. Bunny O'Toole, remember? We met you one day this fall."

She turns away.

"Wait, Jade—*Jane*. Have you seen him? We were skating last night and he just, like, vanished, and I have to find him before—"

She swaps coffeepots around. "Right. If you're his brother—"

"Yeah. Spencer," I say.

"Uh-huh. If you're his brother, you know he's *away*." She turns back. "Next, please."

I wait till she finishes the next order, then plead from beside the donut display, "No, he's not away right now. He's home for ten days on this program, and he has to report in, but he's *gone*. He texted me, but I have to find him before he gets in trouble. I thought he might be here."

She stares at me. Then her face softens, and she smiles a little. "Okay, I remember now. You're Buffalo Boy. Your mom didn't like me much that day."

"Well—"

"Just sayin'. Anyway, Bunny hasn't been here."

"What about the gym?"

"No. I'd have heard. Too hot around there anyway."

A chunky lady with a supervisor's badge hustles past behind the counter. "We need fresh on five and six, Jane."

"On it." Jade or Jane looks at me and shrugs. "Sorry."

"No problem." I pick up my triple-triple, then put it down again and grab a napkin. I've got a pen in a pocket somewhere. "Listen, can I just give you my number? Could you call if you see him?" She nods and I scribble my number on the napkin and pass it to her.

As I turn to go, she says, "If he texted you, can you check the GPS on his phone?"

"Hey," I say, "I never thought of that."

"Jane!" From the supervisor.

"Thanks!" I call. She's already gone.

The first notes of *The Good, the Bad* buzz from my pocket. I put down my cream and sugar with coffee again and check my phone. It's a text from a number I don't recognize. I'd better look, just in case. Maybe Bun's borrowed a phone. What I read is, we got buny trade 4 musik w8 4 contact SPCA.

I think it's time to call Deb.

SEVEN

Deb sounds half asleep when she answers her cell phone. Welcome to the club, I think.

"Is everything all right, hon?"

"I'm not sure," I say. I tell her what's happened.

"Give that to me again, Spence," she says after I read her the SPCA text. Her voice has cleared. I read it off my cell screen again: we got buny trade 4 musik w8 4 contact SPCA. "It sounds as if he's been kidnapped or something. Should I call the cops?"

"No," Deb snaps. Then her tone mellows out. "Listen, Spence, I think you were right before: Bun's met up with some gang kids. Now maybe he's even a little scared to come home. You know his logic isn't always, well, logical. I remember that girl you met. She's covering for them. I've read up on this. Gang people don't trust outsiders."

"Yeah, but I don't even know if she was in the—"

"She had everything but the tattoo," Deb cuts in. She's in full prof mode now. "They also tend to talk in code. That text was from someone else, right?

"Yeah, but—"

"So the others sent it." Her voice is almost cheery now. "They're telling you Bunny's with them, to sit tight and *wait for contact*. It sounds as if they like his iPod too. God knows what he's traded it for. Not another tattoo, I hope."

"Yeah, but who's SPCA? The gang is Fifteenth Street Posse."

Deb gives a teacher-y chuckle. "It's a joke, Spence. SPCA means Society for the Prevention of Cruelty to Animals. They're preventing *cruelty* to a *Bunny*. Get it? It's not half bad."

"Yeah, but—"

"So here's what you do: nothing. I'll deal with this. Stay out of it. Don't call the police. Don't call Roz; I will. Send me her number—it's on the fridge.

Dad's off in his yurt, so you can't reach him anyway."
She's talking fast now. "You did the right thing calling
me. Call me again if you get any more messages, from
anyone. Give Bunny time, and I'll give him hell when
I get home. Don't worry, Spence, it'll all work out.
Now, I've got things to do. And I bet there's a little
tidying you could do."

I pass on that one. "Last thing," I say. "Guess what
happened at the cottage?"

"Spence, I have to run. Aunt Vicki wants me to go
to hot yoga with her. I'll check back with you. Tell me
then. Love you."

It takes three tries to start the van before I can
drive home. I find Roz's number on the fridge under
a skull-shaped Grateful Dead magnet; blame Jer
for that one. I call Deb back, just to hear her voice,
but I get her voice mail instead. Maybe she's found
Roz's number already and she's calling her now.
I leave a message anyway.

The Bun file is now handed off. Life is good again.
I'm meeting AmberLea at one and visiting a megastar.
I'll tell her about what happened at the cottage. We'll
hang out. Maybe Toby will disappear in a Gap store.
There are almost ten days of vacation left, my parents

are away, there are movies to watch and a basement shelf filled with boxes of mac and cheese.

So why am I still weirded out? Deb isn't, and before she left she was all dithery. But maybe she's way ahead of me on this; philosophy profs aren't paid to think life is simple. Or maybe the cruise has totally mellowed her out.

Still, things are nagging at me. Like SPCA: where have I heard that lately? And why would Jade/Jane suggest tracking Bun's phone if she was covering up? And why are Bun's boots here and not his skates? I think about our unlocked door again. Did Bun and the Fifteenth Streeters really make this mess?

Maybe what I need to settle me down is some morning mac and cheese. I'm still hungry; I didn't exactly eat well yesterday. I duck down into the basement to get a box. The light's been left on in Deb's office. I go to turn it off and I freeze. The place is a disaster: cabinets open, drawers dumped, books and papers scattered, the computer light glowing. Deb is a neat freak. Bun and his buds wouldn't have done a food-and-shoe search here. Instantly I'm four years old again, and every shadow is a monster. I zoom upstairs and phone Deb. Voice mail again. I leave a message for her to call me.

Then I go on the shared computer in the den. It takes forever to boot up. I'm panting as I wait. I take a deep, slow breath and go to the website for Bun's phone. The user name and log-in are written on a yellow sticky note on the monitor. I enter and click on the location tab. Up comes a map of Toronto. There's a red dot. It's in the west end, down near the lake—not too far from here. I zoom in closer to look. Then I download the link to my phone, put on my curling sweater and grab the keys to the van.

Stay out of it, Deb said. I have no idea what "it" is, but I don't think staying out is an option anymore—especially when I don't want to stay in here.

EIGHT

The Baby Breeze Motel (*WEEKLY/MONTHLY AC SAT TV VACA CY*) sits crumbling in its parking lot like half a sandwich left at the back of a fridge. I think *skuzzy* is the technical word for this style. The app says Bun's phone is around here. Somewhere.

I was kind of hoping I'd see Bun skating on a frozen puddle or something, but that's not on and he's still not answering either. All I can do is hit the locator tab on the app, walk past the rooms and hope I hear his phone beep.

I turn off the van reluctantly and climb out. It took another three tries to start it for this drive.

I hope it starts when I need to get out of here. It's colder by the lake, and up close, the Baby Breeze isn't exactly homey. Curtains are drawn across every window. The plastic chairs out front are magnets for cigarette butts and empties. Two sorry cars are parked about five doors apart. Both look older than me. One has a flat tire. The O'Toolemobile fits right in.

I hit the button on my phone and start walking, trying to seem like just another wholesome teenager looking for harmless fun at a fleabag motel. A faint beeping kicks in as I pass the second car. It gets stronger every step I take. So does a certain dense, skunky smell I've, uh, smelled before. Both are definitely coming from the end unit. I stop at the door and knock. Nothing; just stink and beeping. "Bun?" I call. "Bunny?" A few rooms back, I think I see a curtain twitch. I ignore it and try the door. It's unlocked. I push it open.

Instantly, the beeping gets louder. Weed stink gushes out on a wave of warm air. Lights are glowing over a small jungle of pot plants on one side of the room. Some kind of foil blanket hangs behind the curtains, duct-taped to the wall, and the carpet is stained. Apart from the plants, the room is empty except for a ratty couch and a shiny pole that runs from floor to ceiling in the middle of the room. One end of a set of handcuffs is clamped around the bottom of the pole. I'm not even going to think about that.

The phone beeps are coming from a kitchenette space behind the couch. "Bunny?" I try again, but I know nobody's home. Get the phone and get out, I think.

I tiptoe fast to the kitchenette. Partway there I wonder why I'm tiptoeing, but I do it anyway. And there's Bun's phone, beeping away on the floor by the counter. I'm just bending for it when I hear a rustling in the leaves behind me and a sound that's a cross between a creaking door and like a bullfrog on steroids. I look over my shoulder. Looking back at me is an alligator.

I don't hear myself scream, but I probably do. I do know that somehow I jump straight up onto the stamp-sized countertop and teeter there, clutching the mini-cabinet fixed to the wall, my head scraping the ceiling.

The gator or crocodile or whatever it is snorts, its black eyes gleaming at me. Its front claws clack and scrabble at the cupboard doors under the counter while its tail thumps the back of the couch. I'm trapped. I could yell for help, but I'm thinking guests at the

Baby Breeze Motel are used to yelling from their neighbors. Cops aren't an option. *Hi, I'm trapped by an alligator in a grow op, and looking for my brother who's skipped his jail pass.* Meanwhile, Bun's phone is still beeping, and I'm starting to feel how hot it is in here.

Clutching the cabinet with one hand, I thumb my cell phone with the other. Then I call the only person who might understand. AmberLea answers on the second ring. "Um, I need some help." My voice only squeaks a little. I tell her what's going on.

"An *alligator?*" she says. I can imagine her chin tucking way in.

"Or a crocodile," I say. "I don't know. But it's one of them and it's big." Below me, there's more snorting and clacking and scrabbling, and then the beeping noise suddenly gets quieter. "And I think it just ate Bun's phone."

"Okay, sit tight," AmberLea says. "We'll think of something. Is there, like, a dogcatcher in Toronto or anything?"

"This isn't a dog!"

"Okay, Animal Control?"

"I dunno. For raccoons, maybe. This thing probably eats raccoons."

"We're on our way."

I don't think about the "we" part. I've got enough on my mind with a hungry crocogator that now beeps, not to mention worries that whoever owns the plants and the pet might show up and find me where I'm not supposed to be.

By the time I finally hear a car pull up out front, I'm drenched in sweat. The place is overheated, and I'm still trapped in my jacket. Plus there's the little matter of being scared: the crocogator is still down below me, waiting. Then car doors slam, and I hear AmberLea's voice. "In there." Footsteps. AmberLea and Toby peer in the doorway.

"Over here," I call as they take it all in.

"Amazing," Toby says. "Plus a stripper pole and handcuffs."

"Where's the gator?" says AmberLea.

"Down there." I point. The crocogator does some huffing and shuffling at the sound of their voices.

"Okay, just stay where you are," AmberLea orders. It's one of those reminders you really don't need. "Give me the bag," she says to Toby.

"No, I'll do it."

"Just give me the bag. We'll argue later."

He hands her a plastic grocery bag. AmberLea steps into the room. Toby comes in behind her, raises a video camera and sweeps the place. AmberLea pulls a family-size package of chicken parts out of it and rips the plastic wrap off. "Here, gatie gatie!" she calls. "Stomp your feet," she orders Toby. She does it too.

The crocogator scuttles around. AmberLea throws a piece of raw chicken just past the couch. The gator oozes forward and the chicken is gone, just like that. The gator gives a prehistoric hiss. "Good girl," AmberLea says. "Have another." She tosses another piece, this time at the open doorway to the bathroom. The gator slides for it, around where a bit of wall sticks out to make a little alcove by the bathroom door. There's a nasty snapping sound. AmberLea heaves more chicken. From the sound of it, it lands in the bathtub. The gator's tail disappears around the corner, and there's a lot of echoey banging and thudding and snorting. "Good for you," AmberLea says. "While you're in there, why not just finish the rest?" She heaves the rest of the chicken parts. I hear various smacks and splats; then Toby dashes past her, and I hear the bathroom door slam shut, trapping the gator.

"Oh, man. Thanks." I more or less melt off the counter.

AmberLea is wiping her hands on the couch.

"Why was that alligator beeping?" she asks.

"It's a long story," I say.

"This isn't the time for *Peter Pan*," Toby says. "Let's get out of here."

NINE

"It must have been a good party," AmberLea says. We're all crowded in the tiny front hall of O'Toole Central. They've followed me back in a Porsche Cayenne with a ski container on top; it only took six tries to start the van. Now we're going to have mac and cheese.

Toby shrugs. "I don't know. By standards in my dorm, a level three." He grins. Perfect teeth. Still, he's eyeing O'Toole Central as if it's as sketchy as the Baby Breeze. I'm also not so crazy about him getting a video shot of me doing a Cowardly Lion on top of a counter, even if the guy did do a primo move slamming that door on the gator. All I say, though, is,

"It wasn't a party. I think somebody searched the place last night while we were at the rink."

"Searched for what?" AmberLea drapes her jacket over the newel post Jer's never finished refinishing. Then she goes and straightens the sofa cushions. She pulls a chip bag and two empty iced-tea tins out from underneath. I don't tell her those are *my* mess from watching movies last night.

"I haven't got a clue," I say, watching Toby arrange his jacket on a hanger. I drop mine on the floor. "They trashed my mom's office too."

I go into the kitchen, stash a mug and two glasses in the sink because the dishwasher's full, then square a pile of DVD cases on the table, on top of where the salt spilled. Now things look tidier.

AmberLea comes in. I heat water in a saucepan and tell them the story, from going skating with Bunny on. Then I show them the texts. "Now I don't know what to think," I finish. "Maybe my mom's right. That motel is pretty close to Posse territory. It could be their grow op. Drugs are their thing."

"So you think Jade was hinting how to find Bunny without ratting anyone out?" AmberLea has pulled her chin in again.

"Maybe." I shrug. The water is boiling. I dump in the macaroni. AmberLea opens drawers until she finds cutlery.

"But that was dangerous," she said. "Would she set you up? Whoever runs that grow op wouldn't have been happy to see you."

"Maybe she tipped them. Maybe she thought they'd be gone, or that only Bun would be there. It looked as if Bun's phone got dropped there by accident."

"But—" She stops. She's just found the plates. "Okay. If Bunny's with Fifteenth Street, why did they search here?"

"Beats me. Just out of habit?" I stir the macaroni with a wooden spoon. "Bun might not have known they searched downstairs." I'm beginning to buy this myself. The mess doesn't seem as sinister with other people around and mac and cheese on the way. "And maybe Bun has shoes I forgot."

"What do you think, T?" AmberLea turns to Toby.

He's sitting at the table, staring at my cell-phone screen.

He murmurs, "SPCA. Maybe we should have called *them* about that alligator."

"It'll be fine," AmberLea says. "I left it lots to snack on." Toby isn't listening. He has his own phone out now, pecking away with his thumbs. The macaroni is ready. I kill the heat, drain the water and open the cheese packets. AmberLea gets milk and butter from the fridge.

"SPCA," Toby says again as I bring the pot of mac and cheese to the table. He reads off his cell screen:

"Society for the Prevention of Cruelty to Animals
Serum Prothrombin Conversion Accelerator
Symposium on Pervasive Computing and Applications
Short Posterior Ciliary Artery
Structural Pest Control Act
Student Paper Competition Award
Security Policy Compliance Assessment
Save Pianvia Counterrevolutionary Army."

"Uh-oh," I say.

TEN

I bring my laptop into the kitchen and show them the bit about the killer in the Pianvia documentary. I tell them what happened at the cottage and how Bunny thinks the killer is our grandpa. Then I show them the text message: we got buny trade 4 musik w8 4 contact SPCA. We do a web search on Pianvia. Wikipedia says:

A tiny, insular Balkan state with a long cultural tradition of cross-dressing. Its economy is built on the export of its national drink, splotnik, a potent liqueur derived from fermented pork rinds.

Little is known for certain about contemporary conditions. A monarchy under King Hoj the 34th until the end of WWI, Pianvia was briefly a democracy until the Nazi invasion of WWII. It was the only state in the region not fully conquered by the Germans in that war, owing to a combination of its geography (impassable mountains and vast tracts of malarial swamp known as yill) and the fierce resistance of partisans led by Josef Josef, a former gym teacher.

Following WWII, Josef established the current People's Paradise of Pianvia (PPP) under his own iron-fisted and eccentric rule and closed the country off entirely. He is known to have banned unicycles, music, films, card tricks, ice cream, television, left-handedness and religions that do not proclaim him a god.

In consolidating his rule, he dealt ruthlessly with political opponents and other dissidents, killing many and forcing others into exile, where they were still not safe from PPP assassins. (See entry for Zoltan Blum.) In a rare appearance at the United Nations in 1959, Josef declared blotzing (killing slowly by chopping into small pieces) Pianvia's new national sport, replacing fleever, a form of polo played by yak-riding warriors who used the skulls of enemies for a ball.

Nominally allied with the Russians during the Cold War, Josef was independent and unpredictable enough to also hold talks with the Americans, who are now known to have been interested in splotnik as a form of chemical weapon and who tried to negotiate a secret trade deal in the 1960s.

Josef Josef died in 1982 and was succeeded by his son, Josef Josef Josef, who is rumored to actually be Josef Josef's daughter, Greta, in disguise. (She has not been seen in public since 1976.) He (or she) has since banned digital technology and massage therapy. Since the fall of the Iron Curtain in the 1990s, opposition to the regime has increased, thanks to the SPCA (Save Pianvia Counterrevolutionary Army), an organization of Pianvian exiles and their descendents based mainly in Canada, the United States and Australia. The SPCA demanded recognition from the UN after a successful armed insurgency left them in control of the Flug Yill Basin in southern Pianvia. They have also enlisted numerous human-rights agencies in their cause, which has gained some popularity. Oprah is rumored to be negotiating a special about their fight, and several low-level Hollywood stars were spotted wearing purple-and-gold SPCA lapel pins at the Academy Awards in 2013.

"So this could be for real. They must have heard about your family from your prof. It's a kidnapping. My god, we have to call the FBI or something." AmberLea is wide-eyed.

"There is no FBI in Canada," I say, "and if we phone somebody, what are we going to tell them? Besides, my mom said not to."

"But all that spy stuff! That guy in the movie could be your grandpa. Your mom didn't know about that."

"Oh, come on. There was no Pianvian passport, and the disguise kit wouldn't even be good enough for Halloween."

"Sounds as if the gun and money would be more than good enough," Toby says.

AmberLea jumps in. "What matters is, it looks as if this SPCA thinks it's him. And if they're for real, and they've snatched Bunny, we need to call the FBI."

"There *is* no FBI in Canada. I just told you that. It would be—"

"So what's this music they want to trade for?" Toby interrupts.

"No idea," I say to him. "Music is banned in Pianvia."

"That Zoltan Blum guy that got killed was a famous composer," AmberLea says. "Do a search."

The Wikipedia entry for Zoltan Blum doesn't help.

(1909-1962) Foremost composer of the tiny Balkan nation of Pianvia. Trained in Vienna, Austria, where he returned following his defection in 1954, after his own country banned music. For much of his career, his work was heavily indebted to Schoenberg and other masters of atonal and serial composition. Too indebted, according to some critics, who made numerous charges of plagiarism, particularly over his "Variations on a Theme for Yak Bells." Manuscripts from his years in exile have disappeared, but he is said to have turned to a simpler and more traditional melodic style, as well as taking up golf, which he described as "fleever on foot."

He died on an Austrian golf course, killed by what was probably an exploding golf ball. Blum is thought to have been one of many victims of assassins working for the notorious Pianvian dictator Josef Josef.

The landline starts ringing. I see the message light is flashing too. The answering machine kicks in before I get to the phone. A canned version of Jerry's voice says, "Hi, thanks for calling O'Toole Central. At the sound of the tone, leave a message for Deb, Jerry, Bunny or Spencer, and we'll get back to you, Scout's honor. And don't forget to wonder what's so crazy about peace, love and understanding." *BEEP.* A voice leaves a message about dentist appointments next week. When it's done, I press *Play* to see who else has called. A familiar voice kicks my eardrums. "Roz Inbow here. Bernard is thirty minutes late for his ten-AM check-in. He needs to call me immediately. I should advise you that there may be consequences."

Oh, no. I look at the wall clock: 11:20. As I do, my cell plays the Bond theme—an incoming call. I don't recognize the number. Maybe it's Bun on a borrowed phone. I answer. A gravelly, accented voice says, "You want Bunny alive, ride 501 East streetcar at noon. Sit in single seat before back doors. Wait for contact from Dusan. Come alone. Or will die like Zoltan Blum." The line goes dead.

ELEVEN

At five minutes to noon, I'm at the Queen Street stop closest to O'Toole Central. There's no one else waiting. AmberLea and Toby are in the Cayenne a block farther along. They'll follow and film the streetcar. I'm shivering. They're probably not, snuggled in their Porsche. I don't have time for that now.

I've never seen a spy movie where the hero takes public transit. Not that I'm a hero. Or that spy movies have much to do with real life. I creep my fingers up into the sleeves of my curling sweater and hug myself. It doesn't help: I'm also shivering because I'm scared and confused. That's not in spy movies either.

How can I convince the SPCA guy meeting me that Grandpa was not a hit man and that the only music he ever owned was for the cheesy Broadway show tunes he banged away at on the piano? But all the time I'm thinking that, I'm also remembering that Wikipedia said Zoltan Blum was blown up by an exploding golf ball, and there *was* that bag of golf balls with funny writing on them in the spy stuff at the cottage. Oh, man.

Down the street I hear the rumble and clang of the streetcar. In Toronto, we call streetcars Red Rockets, which is a joke, because they're slow. Now one rolls up. I climb aboard and drop my fare in the box. There are empty single seats before the back door. I scan every face on the way. There are only a few; none of them scream *SPCA terrorist kidnapper* at me.

Neither do the people who get on at the next stop and filter their way back. I wonder if the pregnant lady is really pregnant. A slender guy in shades, with a full blond beard and mustache, is right behind her. He's got on a long tan coat, a purple-and-gold scarf over top and a leather messenger bag. He's also carrying a full grocery tote. I get a deep vibe that says, *Yurt, Salt Spring Island.* Not really a Bond moment—until Hippie Guy swings into the seat behind me. As the streetcar lurches forward, I hear a familiar gravelly, accented whisper. "Do not turn around."

"From a friend." A hand in a striped woolen glove appears at my side. It's holding Bunny's CRAP ID and a wooly yellow-and-blue hat, just like mine.

"Hey!" I start to turn. Another hand presses my shoulder. "Be still. Low voice. Dusan speaks. We have Bunny. Is good for now." The gloved hand now holds a cell phone. On the screen is a photo of Bunny, holding yesterday's paper. He's smiling. He smiled when they took him to Creekside too. "If you call poliss, not so good. And we will know. We monitor you." The hand rises again. "He is safe return when you get us anthem."

"*What* anthem?" I whisper. "I don't know about music. Look, my grandpa—"

"Your zorga," Dusan growls, "was double agent. Assassin who killed Zoltan Blum, greatest composer of Pianvia."

"No!" I try to turn. The hand clamps my shoulder. I hiss back, "He was a busi—"

"A good cover. He was busy selling much, including talent for killing. Blum knew him as Clint, agent for CIA. Maybe true, maybe he work for others too. In 1962 Blum in Vienna, composing new national anthem for free Pianvia. And was afraid. Knew was being watched clock the round. Clint say CIA will have anthem recorded and played all over world to aid SPCA. Anthem was written only. Blum gave only copy to Clint at golf game. On thirteenth tee, boom, is blown to bits. Most found was ear, in a tree. Bomb in a golf ball. Clint and anthem gone. CIA never get. No one get. Except Clint. Your zorga was Clint. That means you have. We give you twenty-four hours to find and deliver or your brother dies."

"But I…my…"

"Twenty-four hours."

"I don't even know what I'm *looking* for!"

"Listen. Is written by hand, green ink on thick music paper. Is signed with *Z* looking like lightning. This always his way."

"But I don't know where to look," I plead.

"You will think. You knew your zorga. We know is not in your house."

"I *knew* it was searched."

"Voice down, pliss. We'd be surprised if you didn't. All can say is old Pianvian proverb: best place to hide splotnik is in plain sight."

"But what if it got thrown out? Or lost?"

"Your zorga would not. He knew was value to many people, that he might need for deal one day."

I don't know what to say. Or do. All I can do is blurt, "I found Bunny's cell phone at your grow op. The crocogator ate it."

"Vhat?" Dusan's voice cracks upward. "Grow op? Croco…?" Then it hits gravel bottom again. "You have shock, shake-up maybe. Is okay. We toss Bunny's cell phone on street after first message—could be traced. Anybody could get. Sound like someone else did. But you clever boy, Spencer, you find. That means you will find anthem. Think careful; time short. Now, take out phone and enter ziss number." The gloved hand floats in front of me again, with the cell phone. I punch the number on the screen into my log. "Call second you find anthem. Brother Bunny home sooner and world will hear music that rally to our cause. You do great thing, Spencer. You help free a people and save us blotzing Bunny."

I know what blotzing means. The streetcar is slowing. I haven't even noticed we've been moving all this time. How many stops have we come? "I leave now," Dusan growls. "No look, no follow. In building we stop at is man waiting, with AK-47. He watches for you. If you even turn before car starts again, he fires, at everyone on street but you. You we need. You don't need be cause for more deaths."

There's a little jerk as the streetcar stops, then the hydraulic *whoosh* of the doors opening. "Damn," comes a woman's voice from somewhere behind me, "I forgot bananas." Then it's all feet scuffling and tramping, and I know no one's there.

I'm frozen. My whole body is screaming to turn around, stand up, run after him, signal AmberLea and Toby, anything. I can't take the chance. But I can text AmberLea: beard shades purple gold scarf bag. The instant the car starts, I'm running to the back window. I catch a flash of purple and gold, and blond hair in a low ponytail, then it's gone. I pull the bell cord and dive off at the next stop. I run back, full out. I pass the Cayenne and keep running, dodging strollers and striders and a lady walking four dogs. Ahead I see a corner grocery. A sign in the window says, *BANANAS 49*. The store is closed. Whoever Dusan is, he's gone.

TWELVE

Toby and AmberLea drive me home. I tell them what happened. AmberLea has filmed everyone getting off at each stop. She huddles with me in the backseat and we watch. There's not much to see: the guy climbs off behind some other people, shades on and fumbling with something at his mouth. Then someone gets in the way and he's moving out of the frame, with the scarf pulled up to his nose. Then he's gone. "I wish you'd texted me earlier." AmberLea sighs.

I tell them about the sniper threat. AmberLea groans. "That's right out of *Die Job Four*. Don't you remember? Bruce Willis, Nicole Kidman—"

"And Christopher Walken, 2006," Toby finishes for her.

I don't remember. I should remember, but right now all I can think is, *This is for real* as I punch Deb's number into my phone. She's still not picking up. I leave another message.

"I wonder whose grow op you stumbled into," Toby says as he parks behind the family van.

"It doesn't matter." I stuff my phone into my pocket and pop the seat belt. "It doesn't even matter that my grandpa might not be the killer. They think he is. What if he isn't? There won't be any music. They'll kill Bunny."

"FBI," says AmberLea. "No, I mean RCMB or whoever."

"*No.* He said no cops. And they're watching me. They're probably watching us right now."

"Okay, okay, calm down." AmberLea presses her hands down on my knees to keep them from bouncing. "You're doing an Angry Bird here. He told you to think carefully, right? Okay, let's think. For now, we have to go with your grandpa as the guy, right? We have to look for the music, just in case. Maybe it'll buy time, if nothing else. So, where do we look?"

"Well, Grandpa's stuff was all split up when we sold his house. We got his piano and music, but the anthem's not here; the guy said so himself. The only other place is the cottage. There's an old piano there, too, and music."

"And all the spy stuff was there," AmberLea puts in.

"So I've got to go back to the cottage. Now." I jump out of the Cayenne, run to the house, grab the keys, race back out and hop in the van. I'm in overdrive.

Unfortunately, the O'Toolemobile is not. This time it won't start at all. I slam the steering wheel with my hand. The horn starts beeping. I yell and slam the wheel again. This does not help. AmberLea taps on the window. I crank it down.

"Spence," she says over the horn, "we'll drive you."

Toby reaches in to the key ring and presses the alarm button. The horn stops. "Sometimes that works." He grins.

I take a couple of breaths to slow down. "Okay," I say, climbing out. "Let's go."

"Deal," says AmberLea. "Right after we go see Aiden Tween."

THIRTEEN

One of my profs told us that a lot of movie stars are short people with big heads—I mean, literally big heads—and that the women are all skinny as rails. The camera makes you look twenty pounds heavier, and big heads photograph better for some reason. The rest is camera angles, lighting and standing on milk crates.

I think of this because the first thing I notice about Aiden Tween, in the royal suite of the hotel, is how *tiny* he is. Except for his head. His head is huge. This may be because he's wearing a gigantic old-time gangster hat on top of oversized aviator shades and brick-sized headphones. The headphones are plugged into an electronic keyboard he's soundlessly plunking on. He's facing a giant flat screen that's been set up in front of the drawn curtains, showing something in black and white.

His manager, Sumo, leads us in. We've surrendered all our electronics—so much for my *cinema verité* idea. Then we signed forms promising not to blab about anything we see or hear or to sue if we fall out a window or break a fingernail or anything. Sumo's all in black, which makes his bling and his head look even shinier. He's chewing gum like a cartoon beaver gnaws a log. His words spit out like wood chips. "AT's got a big meet, then a rehearsal. Ten minutes only." That's fine with me.

AmberLea nods and nudges Toby. Toby's taken his dumb wooly hat off. He gives his hair a careless brush that somehow makes it perfect. I push up my glasses. I remind myself that Aiden Tween is a teeny-bopper joke. I remind myself I'm on a mission to save Bunny. I'm nervous anyway.

Sumo hustles across an acre of white carpet, scoops a remote and freezes the image on-screen. Aiden Tween stops playing piano. "Aw, stink," he whines in a Southern accent. "It was just comin' to my favorite part."

"Good. Something to look forward to." Sumo grunts. "Your invited guests, AT."

"AmberLea," AmberLea calls. "Gloria Lorraine's granddaughter."

AT has pried up an earpad in time for the last bit. He lights up, as much as you can behind a hat, shades and headphones. "Riiiiight." He pulls off the hat and phones. Somehow, his head looks even bigger without them. His hair is slicked back perfectly in the giant upsweep I've seen in photos lately. It's his new look. How does he keep it that way under a hat and headphones? Maybe Toby knows. "See what I'm watchin'?" AT nods at the screen, where I now see a young Gloria Lorraine, AmberLea's grandma, frozen with one hand reaching into her purse. Gloria Lorraine was a babe when she was in movies.

"Hey, that's *Blond Trust*," AmberLea burbles.

"Right on," says Aiden Tween. He cackles behind his shades. It's a rising sound, as if he's sucking in helium.

"1949," Toby says casually, "with Richard Widmark and Edward G. Robinson."

"Right *on*," AT squeaks again. He pulls off the aviator shades and looks at Toby. "Hey, nice scarf."

"Hat goes with it." Toby holds it up and steps forward. He sounds as if he talks to world-famous people every day. For all I know, maybe he does.

"Sweet," says Aiden Tween. "I gotta get me one." He walks toward a couch bigger than our living room. "C'mon in. Set down." He swings a flashy-looking guitar off the couch and plunks himself down on one end. "So you're—"

"Toby," says Toby. He lounges into a chair the size of a hot tub. "And this is Spencer, and this is AmberLea. *She's* the granddaughter." Everybody laughs as if this is a killer joke.

"Hey." Aiden Tween nods at me, then turns to AmberLea. "Man, Gloria Lorraine's granddaughter? How cool is that? She's my all-time favorite. I'm into old stuff, you know. That's my thing. Hey, guess what this is that I'm wearin'?" He stretches his little arms wide. He's in a dark gray, chalk-striped double-breasted suit. Underneath it is a black T-shirt and a gold necklace with a tiny pair of sneakers set in his Comet Shuffle move. The suit is a little too big. Sticking out from the cuffed pants are orange-and-black padded high-tops. Before anyone can answer, he crows, "It's Humphrey Bogart's suit from *The Maltese Falcon*! I got it at an auction in New York last week. I still gotta get it altered, and it itches like a bugger, but I'm wearin' Bogart's suit! Biggest star of all time! Is that cool or what?"

We nod that it's cool. I've got nothing to say except *can we go now?* and the answer to that is no. Toby, on the other hand, seems right at home. He reaches out to feel the fabric on one sleeve. "Nice," he says and starts talking about the cut. AmberLea sits on the couch and they all start blabbing away. Some other time, this would be so weird it would be fascinating. I'd want to tell Bun all about it. Right now I'd be happy to tell Bun anything.

I'm too wound up to sit, so I wander. A giant security guy with an earpiece watches me from by the door. I try to look innocent for the second time today. Behind me, Aiden Tween is blathering about hot-air balloons and pirate ships. Sumo is in and out of the room, texting and barking into a cell phone. Other people bustle around in the background.

The keyboard is hooked to a laptop with lines of music on the screen. I look at the video games, pinball machine, drum kit, the framed poster showing a close-up shot of feet in gold skate shoes, again in the Comet Shuffle, and above them in big letters:

where it's
AT

I walk to a sideboard with a spread of fruit and junk food and energy drinks. In front of it, there's a big table set up for a meeting. There are printouts at each place.

Transitioning AT
GOAL: broaden AT appeal to 18-35 market
OPTIONS

- Sponsor Formula One racing team
- Photo op with Dalai Lama/Pope (see below)
- Film offers
- Duets album (Madonna, Mick, Beyoncé, Gaga, Sting, Tony Bennett, Kanye)
- Spokesman for worthy causes
  - Domestic:
    - organ donation
    - pet dignity: ban on exploitive cat/dog videos
  - International:
    - world peace
    - substandard synthetic wig hair
    - child labor / 3rd world work conditions
    - music for Pianvia
    - free Tibet (see Dalai Lama above)

"Hey," I blurt, "Pianvia." Heads turn.

"Get away from there," snaps Sumo. The security guy starts to move. "Never mind. Who laid that out? Too early."

A girl hurries over. Her yellow jeans may be sprayed on. She glares at me, then starts scooping papers.

"Sorry," I say. She ignores me. I stare at her jeans anyway.

"Spencer has Pianvia on the brain right now," AmberLea says to AT.

"Right on." AT nods, he jumps up and lopes over, Humphrey Bogart's suit flapping on him like a sail in the wind. His teeth gleam. His hair doesn't move at all. He's a living bobblehead worth a hundred million dollars who dances, sings, plays instruments and writes songs while watching old movies. When I'm on my game, I can open a soda tin and put dip on a chip while watching a movie. He snatches one of the papers from the girl. "Y'all really know about Pianvia?"

I nod. I'm not sure how much to say. It's also odd for me to look down at someone older than me. "One of my film profs is making a documentary about it."

"Get out! That's fantastic. You hear that, Sumo?" Sumo waves one hand. He's texting with the other. "A doc, huh?" AT bounces in his high-tops as he talks. "I wanna see that. How long is it? Can he send me highlights? I don't always have a lot of time."

"Time" comes out "tahm."

"That Pianvia though," AT goes on. "You know they banned *music*? Only country in the world's never heard me, guaranteed. Man, I wanna change that. They deserve music. Hey, they deserve me! They need to be Tweeners! Maybe he could make a doc about me."

Before I can say anything, AT has wheeled to the couch, waving the sheet of paper. "There's just so much injustice in the world, you know? Y'all know how making synthetic wig hair for cheap is cutting into the market for buying Third World—is that the right world, Sumo?—real hair for wigs? Man, the hair harvest has been cut in half! We gotta help!"

"Absolutely." Sumo pockets his phone and rumbles forward. "We'll talk about it as soon as these folks leave. It's time. 'Preciate your dropping by," he says to us.

AmberLea and Toby stand up. Toby nudges her. "We brought you something," he says.

AmberLea starts. "Right! I almost forgot. It's really funny that you were watching that"—she nods at the flat screen, where Gloria Lorraine is still reaching into her purse—"because I brought you these. It was Toby's idea, really." She reaches into her own bag. Instantly, the security guy is at her elbow. AT waves him back.

AmberLea unfolds a pair of white gloves from a small plastic bag and hands them to AT. "She wore these in that movie," AmberLea says. "I think she takes them out of her purse in this scene."

"Gimme the remote," AT says. Sumo hands it to him. He presses a button. Gloria Lorraine springs to life and, sure enough, pulls a pair of white gloves from her bag. For a second it looks as if she's about to put them on. Then she slaps Edward G. Robinson across the face with them.

"Right *on!*" AT does his helium cackle again. "And these are the gloves. How cool is that! Thanks, man." And with that, he pulls one on. It fits. "Look at that. Gloria Lorraine's glove that hit Edward G. Robinson. Man oh man. Know what I'm gonna do? I'm gonna wear these for my New Year's Eve show. You coming? You've gotta be there. Sumo, put them on the list.

All access, after-party. Gotta be." Sumo nods. AT gives AmberLea a hug. "Careful of the suit," he warns. "Send me the pictures, okay?" he says to AmberLea, then waves at me. "And send me that movie." He turns to speak to Toby, who's lagged behind. Sumo is practically shoving AmberLea and me to the door. He calls to a helper, "All access for these folks. Get their names." To me, he murmurs, "You really know Pianvia?"

"Yeah, I—"

"Big stuff?"

"Oh, yeah."

"How old are you?"

"Eighteen." This will be true next month.

"Huh. Could be trending. Send *me* the movie. And call me when you do. Make sure I get it. Schedule's tight. Decisions. High priority." He shoves a card in my hand. "Call me." Toby catches up. Sumo shuts the door behind us.

FOURTEEN

"Whew." AmberLea sags as we ride the private elevator down from about the three hundredth floor. "We just met a teeny-tiny megastar."

I shrug and watch the floor lights blink down. I want to say, "teeny-tiny bobblehead," but I don't.

Toby says, "Now that I've met him, I feel kind of sorry for him. He was poor as dirt when he was little, never got to go anywhere, and now he's trapped up there with his entourage and never sees anything."

"I suppose." AmberLea giggles a little. "Good call on the gloves. It looks like we have a plan for New Year's, guys. Partying backstage with Aiden Tween."

"Game on," says Toby, giving her a secret little smile.

"Have fun," I mutter. "I might be a little busy trying to save Bun."

"Aw, Spence." AmberLea reaches for my arm as the elevator slows.

"That's another thing," Toby points out unhelpfully as the doors open. "He knew about Pianvia. That's more than we did yesterday. He even wants to help them."

"I don't think the SPCA needs any help," I say. We step into the lobby.

AmberLea tucks her chin in. "Why did you mention Pianvia up there, Spencer? I thought this was secret."

"It was on some papers on the table. They're trying to find ways to make AT cool for an older audience. Anyway, let's go. It's one thirty already."

"I thought he was awesome when I was thirteen," AmberLea says, catching up. I know she's not talking about Bunny. Before I can say anything, a flash of purple and gold catches my eye, along with a streak of blond hair and a patch of tan coat, disappearing behind a mirrored pillar across the lobby.

I dodge a bellhop pushing a roller rack full of luggage, hurdle a dog-carrier cage and skid around the pillar, screeching to a stop a nanosecond before I slam into a slender woman with a blond ponytail, wearing a purple-and-gold scarf over her tan coat. She's got her earbuds in, calmly dialing up some tunes on her cell phone. Beyoncé, I'm guessing. No, maybe Dixie Chicks. Anyway, she's got grade-two teacher written all over her. She looks up as I manage a "Whoa, sorry."

"No worries." She smiles. It's a clear, calm grade-two-teacher voice. She heads out the revolving door, leaving me thinking that life was simpler in grade two. I bet she'd have a Band-Aid for me in her messenger bag if I needed it.

FIFTEEN

We're way ahead of the rush hour, and holiday traffic is light anyway, so it isn't long before AmberLea has the Cayenne headed up Highway 400. She's called her mom, Tina, and told her that the three of us are going to a megamall north of the city and will meet her at the hotel for dinner at seven thirty. With two hours to get to the cottage, an hour to search the place and two hours to drive back, we should just make it.

The mention of dinner reminds us that we're hungry though. We stop for food and gas at a highway place south of Barrie. "Hey," AmberLea says, "isn't this where—?"

"Yup," I say. We stopped here last summer on our road trip with Gloria Lorraine. Today, a lot of the cars have ski racks and gear on top. The Cayenne fits right in. "This is where you saved our lives the first time."

"*Whaat?*" Toby asks from the backseat. I'd made sure to call shotgun.

"A trick with a dog, a cop and a GPS," I say. "Ever see *Red Means Go*? Matt Damon, Angelina Jolie?"

"No." Good, I think.

"From 2008," Amberlea chimes in. "With Jeff Bridges too. I'll tell you about it later." That means *when Spencer's not around.* Bad, I think.

We get to the cottage just after four and ease down the lane. I see an SUV at the neighbors' place. Their cottage lights are already glowing. I figure we have about half an hour of daylight left to make searching easier. Whether there's anything to find is another question.

We trudge in over yesterday's footprints. I find the key behind the thermometer on the wall and we tromp into the kitchen, snow on our feet. I throw the breaker, and the lights lift the dimness. Underneath the cold you can smell the cottage, waiting to come to life. I'm not sure what else is about to come to life, except I know it won't be good.

I lead them into the main room. "Wow," AmberLea says, "this is so cool. It *is* a lot like Gloria's cottage." Her tone darkens. "Which Aiden Tween says…oh, never mind. Let's get at this. What are we after? Where do we start?"

I describe the sheet of music. "There're music books in the piano bench, and we should check in here, where the spy stuff was." I go to the wall, clear some of the wood we left and tug the compartment open.

"I'll start there," says Toby. "Fresh eyes. AmberLea, the piano bench. Spencer knows the place, so he roves."

I'm starting to hate it when Toby makes good suggestions. I nod anyway.

Where *do* you start? How do you hide something in plain sight? What haven't I seen? Everything here is the way it was when *my mom* was little. The Muskoka Dairy calendar (*WE MOO FOR YOU*) on the back of the kitchen door is from 1965, for crying out loud. I look behind it: nothing. I look in kitchen cupboards, behind photos and pinned-up little-kid artwork and painting reproductions. I look under the pad on the ironing board. I look under mattresses, behind mirrors, on the bottoms of chairs and tables and drawers, up in the porch rafters. I look behind pennants from places like Old Fort Henry and Upper Canada Village. By now it's black outside the windows. I don't want to find anything here, but I don't want Bunny to die. I keep on looking.

All that's left is Grandpa's bedroom. His fishing hat is still hanging from the mirror frame, lurking with the ghost of his aftershave. DJ slept here when we came up; he's left sweat socks behind. I move as if I shouldn't be in here, as if Grandpa might step in from the porch and catch me. What would he have done if he did? I feel like a spy just wondering if he was. Across the room, something flickers. I spin to see myself in the window glass. I take a deep breath. This is *Grandpa* we're talking about here: Road Runner cartoons, big hugs, LEGO on your birthday, swimming off the dock.

The closet and dresser are empty. Deb and my aunts cleared everything out and gave most of it to the Goodwill. I wonder if I could persuade the SPCA that maybe the music got thrown out then, because nobody knew what it was.

I check under the drawers and mattress and in the bedside table. Nothing. The headboard of the bed has a bookshelf built in, lined with tattered old cottage paperbacks. There are a couple of James Bonds and a lot of other spy stuff: *Eye of the Needle, The Spy Who Came in from the Cold, The Ipcress File, Tinker Tailor Soldier Spy, Funeral In Berlin*…Grandpa had a little theme running here. The spy stories are propped upright by a bigger, thicker book lying on its side. *The Anatomy of Melancholy*. I'm feeling pretty melancholy myself. I bump it off the shelf, reaching in behind to see if the music's there. The book falls to the bed and out tumbles a Colt .45 automatic, the kind I've seen in a million World War II movies. A space for it has been hollowed out in the pages. I gasp, then scoop up the gun and shove it in my pocket. I slam the book back onto the shelf, back out of the room and kill the light.

SIXTEEN

Back in the main room, AmberLea is still flipping through piano music. Toby's poking around inside the piano. He looks up. "Nothing. No secret compartment behind the secret compartment either. I looked in the gramophone too." There's a wind-up gramophone beside me. I lean on it to hide my trembling. The gun clunks against it. I flinch. I don't know why I don't want them to know about the gun, but I don't. Somehow it makes things worse. As if he can read my mind, Toby says, "And there was no Walther PPK."

"What?" I scuttle to the compartment to peek in, hoping the Colt .45 doesn't make my sweater sag too much. Toby's right: no PPK, which means I'm not the only McLean grandson on the loose with an automatic weapon. *Good luck at those airports, guys.* Right now, I've got more pressing issues.

Toby says gently, "Couldn't help noticing those, uh, weird golf balls though. There's one short of an even dozen."

I swallow hard. I can't look at anyone. I figure we're all thinking about how Zoltan Blum was killed. Now for sure I don't want them to know about the gun I just found. "Yeah," I say at last. "I think they're Cuban. My grandpa ran an import/export business. You should have seen the wooden Frisbees from Australia."

There's an awkward silence. AmberLea breaks it by tossing another music book aside. "Zilch. Didn't your grandpa like any music but Broadway shows?"

"Well, Christmas carols. And old dance-band stuff he played on the gramophone here." I move back to the gramophone to show a rack of ancient 78 rpm records. It's such a relief to talk about something else that I can't stop. "His rule was no electronics. We'd wind up the gramophone at drinks before dinner, or he'd play piano for singalongs. Jer brought his guitar sometimes, but Grandpa wasn't into that so much."

I close the gramophone cabinet. "Once, Deb—my mom—snuck a portable radio in when she was a kid, and Grandpa found it and said the only place she could listen to it was in the outhouse. 'Elvis belongs in the outhouse,' he'd say. All rock was Elvis to Grandpa. Me and my cousins used to sneak iPods up, and if he caught us he'd say the same thing to us." I stop. I'm drifting into thoughts I don't want. I didn't always like coming to the cottage. It was a place for the physical guys like Bunny and DJ and Adam. I was always afraid I'd get thrown in the lake, or get a lap full of water at dinner. That's another story too.

"You still use an outhouse?" AmberLea interrupts my thoughts. Her chin has done its disappearing act.

"No, no. Just for backup. The bathroom's down the hall."

AmberLea jumps up.

"Except the water's not on," I say.

She stops. "Well, what did you guys do? It's kinda urgent, you know?"

I get it. "We brought water with us and poured it down the toilet."

"Great. Where's the water?"

"We didn't bring any today."

"So what are my options? Quickly."

"Um, well, I guess go in the snow or use the outhouse. DJ used the outhouse. He said it was like being back on Kilimanjaro."

"Super." AmberLea sighs. "Where is it?"

"Out back." She hustles to the kitchen door. I flick on the outside light. The biffy stands by some leafless bushes, a half moon cut in the top part of the door. You can still see DJ's size 13 footprints leading to and from it.

"Oh man, Spencer." AmberLea sighs again. "You're gonna owe me big-time." She grabs the flashlight from Toby.

"There probably won't be spiders this time of year," he says.

"And it won't smell bad," I add.

"Double super." AmberLea gives us a fake smile and a bit of sign language involving one finger. She opens the door. "Well, at least come outside so you'll hear me if I scream. And there'd better be T.P. in there."

Toby and I follow her outside. Strangely, it feels slightly warmer out there than it does in the cottage. AmberLea mashes her way through the snow and wrestles the door open. The flashlight plays on the inside of the biffy.

"What's all over the walls?" asks Toby.

"Old cartoons and covers from the *New Yorker*," I say. "I think I have them memorized. My grandpa had a subscription." The door bangs shut behind AmberLea. "And a picture Deb—my mom did when she was little, like five or six."

"Your grandpa hung it in the biffy?"

"That's what it was for. It's of flowers. My mom said it would make the place smell better."

"You have an interesting family," says Toby.

"You don't know the half of it."

A moment later the door bangs open and AmberLea high-steps back through the snow. "There's a kid's drawing on the door in there," she says. "Of flowers."

"Yeah, I was just telling Toby that my mom did that."

"Ever notice it's on music manuscript paper? Maybe we should look on the other side."

Deb's crayon drawing of a vase of flowers is stuck to the outhouse door with rusting thumbtacks. It takes some work to pry them out. It's a regular-sized sheet of paper, but almost as heavy as cardboard and yellowed with age and outhouse life in general. Deb may have skipped two grades in primary school, but I bet she failed Art. She couldn't even color inside her own lines. I've been looking at this all my life, every time we played hide-and-seek at the cottage or needed a last-minute pee before hitting the highway, and it's only now, with the flashlight trained on it, that I notice the sets of five lines stretching across the paper.

I flip the page over. On the other side, music, complicated-looking music, has been written into the lines. The green ink has faded, but the penmanship is sure and sharp. Below the music, what I guess are lyrics have been printed in more of that Russian-style writing. In the corner is a bold lightning bolt of a *Z*.

"Bingo," breathes AmberLea.

SEVENTEEN

"So," Tina says when we're all sitting down, "Aiden Tween. Tell me everything."

We're at a table for four at Yueh Tung, a Chinese restaurant I know on Elizabeth Street, just behind city hall. Tina is AmberLea's mom. I haven't seen her since September. She still has the same tan.

Yueh Tung is pretty big. The place is busy. The waiter brings tea. AmberLea pours. Toby talks. I'm so tired and mixed-up I can barely listen. I haven't processed anything since we found the music on the outhouse wall. It was all I could do to think of this place when Tina suggested Chinese; Yueh Tung is an O'Toole standard.

I'm waiting to hear *The Good, the Bad*. I've messaged the number Dusan gave me and sent a photo of the lightning-bolt *Z*. The anthem is nestled underneath my shirt in the Muskoka Dairy calendar. My phone is in one pocket of my curling sweater, along with Grandpa's silly disguise kit. The Colt automatic is in the other. AmberLea and Toby don't know I have those things. I don't know *why* I have them, and now I feel stupid, as if I'm wearing a *CONCEALED WEAPON* sign. I wonder if I can share a room with Bunny if I end up in Creekside. I wonder which cousin is packing the PPK. Maybe he'll join us.

Now I order barbecued pork and bean curd, like always. The others are talking about Aiden Tween. Toby has turned into quite the motormouth. You can tell by the way Tina listens and laughs that she thinks Toby is just the right rich, preppy type for AmberLea. This does not make me feel better, but it's the least of my worries right now. I sip some tea as AmberLea gets into the conversation. "But you know what he's going to do? He's going to tear down all the cottages he bought, including Grandma's—except for her chimney,

88

which he's going to build into the screening room in his, whatever, private theme-park palace with a giant water-slide and a launchpad for his hot-air balloon. He wants to buy a pirate ship to sail around the lake in. How gross is that? He'll wreck everything that's nice up there."

Tina shrugs. "Things change, sweetie. No point in getting sentimental over a place you only went to once and that Grandma never used. We didn't even know it existed until last summer." She sips some tea. "And Aiden Tween is paying you hundreds of thousands of dollars to do what he wants with it. Be thankful Grandma left you the place. It's not a little nest egg, it's a big one. More than she did for me."

"'The very rich are different from you and me,'" Toby intones. "*The Great Gatsby*."

AmberLea sighs. "Yeah, but still. I mean, Spencer's grandpa's cottage has been added to without—" She breaks off. Tina isn't supposed to know about today's road trip.

Tina doesn't seem to notice. She starts asking me about my parents and saying it's too bad they're away right now. "And how's—is it Bunny? How's he doing where he, uh…" Tina doesn't want to say Bun's in jail, I guess.

"Good," I say. "He's home for the holidays. Visiting with other people tonight. I'm kind of hoping they'll call, actually." On cue comes the Bond theme. I pull out my phone. It's Deb.

"Spencer!"

"Mom, I've got to—stuff has happened." I look up. Everyone at the table is looking at me, especially Tina.

AmberLea jumps in. "Wow, am I ever hungry. All that shopping, you know?"

Tina turns to AmberLea. "What did you get?"

"Excuse me," I say to them, then "Just a sec" into the phone. I'll let AmberLea dig her own way out of the shopping lie. I get up from the table, trying not to bump the Colt around, then hustle through the dining room to the stairs. The wig, or maybe the beard, is poking out of my pocket from when I grabbed my phone. I stuff it back out of sight. "Mom," I say, "it's going crazy around here. Bunny's been—"

"Spence"—Deb has gone into Patient Professor mode—"I told you, I'm on this. Bunny will be fine. This SPCA thing—"

"It's not a joke," I break in. "I met one of them." I blurt out how I met Dusan on the 501 and then I tell her the basics of what happened afterward. Deb mutters patient *Uh-huh*s for most of it, along with a couple of *Oh, for crying out loud*s. She does perk up at the Aiden Tween part, though. "*Aiden Tween? The singer?* What's he got to do with this?" I explain about Gloria Lorraine's cottage. "He knows about Pianvia too."

"Well, hon, the Pianvian freedom movement has been getting good press lately. There was a seminar and a rally at the university."

"Why haven't I ever heard of it?"

"There are better news sources than Facebook, Spence. Anyway, I'm sure that's why Bun's friends have picked up on it."

"I thought you said SPCA was about animal cruelty to Bunny."

"I did. Then I remembered this Pianvia thing. You've confirmed it."

"So you still think this is all a goof? What about the music we found?"

"You know what, hon? I remember drawing that picture of flowers for the outhouse, because everyone thought the idea was so funny. Grandpa gave me the piece of paper I used from scraps in the kindling basket.

It was probably a travel souvenir he got tired of. If it was really valuable, do you think he'd have had it in there?"

"I guess not."

"Bingo," says Deb. "Maybe Bun told them about it to send you on a treasure hunt. You know his sense of humor. Frankly, I still think they're after his iPod. So how about this: you do whatever it is they want you to do. Play along, if it makes you feel better. Keep me posted. Is Bun answering his phone?"

"No, it got swallowed by an alligator. Or a crocodile."

"Pardon?"

"It got—never mind. He doesn't have his phone. They gave me a number to call." I give it to Deb.

"I'll try it," says Deb. "I wouldn't be surprised if it belongs to that girl we met at Creekside that time."

"No," I say, "she's how I found the alligator."

"Of course," Deb says. "Moving right along, how was cottage time with the cousins?"

"It got cut short. We found all this stuff in the wall. Passports, money, disguises, a—"

"Oh, Spencer! That was Grandpa's espionage game. He used to play that with grown-up guests back in the 60s, when I was little. Why did that cut it short?"

"Well," I say, "DJ went to England, Adam's in the Carribean, and Webb went back to Nashville."

"*What?*"

Instantly, I know I've blown it. I've ratted them out. "Don't tell their moms."

"Spencer," Deb asks, "you weren't all drinking a lot or anything? Were there drugs? Hallucinogens? You can tell me. Dad and I will understand. It's an age thing—experimenting, pushing boundaries."

"Are you nuts?" I say. "DJ barely drinks milk."

"Fine, fine. Where are you now?" I tell her about dinner at Yueh Tung.

"Good," Deb says. "Stay in touch with them. Call me anytime; keep me up to date. Just relax."

"You forgot to call Roz," I say.

"I'm on it," Deb says. "Promise. Got to run. Love you. 'Bye."

I walk back to the table. Our food has just arrived.

"Spencer," Tina says to me, "it's all decided. Here's the plan. Tomorrow, you're coming skiing with us. AmberLea says you're waiting on a call; you can take it there."

"I don't know how to ski," I say.

"There's always a first time."

I'm learning that. I pull out my chair, and my sweater clunks against the leg—the gun. And Deb almost had me convinced. I don't know what's going on, but I do know I just may be on my own.

EIGHTEEN

After dinner, Toby, AmberLea and Tina are going to a new zombie movie. I beg off. All at once, I'm so out of it that I just want to go home. It also occurs to me that if somehow Mom is right and Bun's just lost his phone, he might not remember my cell number. That would mean he'd call O'Toole Central.

As we leave, I slip the calendar with the music inside it to AmberLea, to put in the hotel safe. "Oooh, vintage collectible," says Tina. "You found that at the mall?"

"Little place north of the city," I say and start for home.

"Ten o'clock tomorrow," Tina calls. I wave.

I ride the 501 Red Rocket home and shuffle down Tecumseth Street to O'Toole Central. As I turn in at our place, fumbling for my key, there's a rustling in the bushes. I'm knocked to the ground. I gasp and try to scramble up. A knee, or something, slams into my back, driving me down again. "Stay down and you won't get hurt." The weight crushes my back. I can barely breathe. Hands rake my legs, feel under my sweater. One brushes the wig and cell phone in my sweater pocket and moves on. I have the gun jammed painfully under my hip. The hand doesn't check there. Instead, it grips my head, forcing it down. "Where is it?" The voice is harsh, panting.

"Not…here," I gasp. "Someplace…safe." My cheek grinds against the frozen dirt. My glasses are half off. Somewhere close by, a car starts up. It needs to visit one of the Mimico muffler-repair places I passed early this morning. The hands let go. Footsteps slap away. I roll over and fumble my glasses on in time to see the passenger door slam on an old gray Honda Civic. It roars away, one side of the rear bumper sagging. I stagger to the house.

NINETEEN

Inside, I lock the door and sag against it for a minute, until my shaking stops. My palms are raw. The hall mirror shows a scrape on my jaw. My back and hip throb where a knee and the Colt crunched them. I limp to the kitchen and try to clean my hands and face. I'm as much of a mess as the house.

I check the landline for messages. There's only one: Roz Inbow. "Three fifteen PM. Bernard is now in violation of his terms of release. If he does not check in by five PM this afternoon, a warrant will be issued for his arrest. Don't let this happen." *CLICK*. Well, that's Deb's problem, and maybe the least of

Bun's right now. Is kidnapping by terrorists an okay excuse for missing your parole call? If I were Bun, I'd be looking forward to jail right now.

I'm exhausted, but I'm so creeped-out I can't sit still. So I do something unheard of: I tidy up. A little. With the last of my energy, I clear the kitchen, scrub the mac-and-cheese pot, crank the dishwasher. Then I tidy up the living room. The last thing I do is put the Colt in the cookie jar, with what's left of Jer's shortbread. I haven't watched all six seasons of *The Rockford Files* for nothing. It's one of the few things Grandpa and I had in common.

By then I'm zonked. I check the door locks, crash on the couch and fire up my laptop. Except for my scraped jaw, I don't hurt anymore. My cell phone is beside me in case they call, but I need a movie to shut out the craziness for a little while. Maybe I should have gone to the zombie flick. I don't like to think about AmberLea and Toby snuggled down side by side in the Eaton Centre Cineplex, even if Tina is with them. I'd have made sure to sit between them. *Aargh.* Now I really need a movie. I've already watched the old Bonds and the Austin Powers movies, and of course the Bourne movies and the *Mission: Impossibles*. I choose a movie with the same title as one of the books I saw in Grandpa's bedroom: *The Ipcress File*.

Maybe it's a bad choice: it starts with a kidnapping. Then I start to get into it. It's from the 60s, but the main character, Harry Palmer, is nothing like Bond. Harry wears glasses with black frames, like my new ones, and he has a low-class Brit accent. I've seen the actor—Michael Caine—before, in newer movies.

When I get to the part where the foreign bad guys kidnap him and try to brainwash him with cheesy whirling lights, I think: he could be in Pianvia. Harry stays focused by grinding his wrists against the restraining straps till he bleeds and secretly jabbing his palm with a piece of wire. Could I do that? Not in a million years. What would Bun say if they interrogated him? He could take it. And Bun thinks differently. He's smart, but not school smart. Other people don't always get his answers. Sometimes it gets him into trouble. Sometimes people don't get it until it's too late. Now, on-screen, Harry has escaped. He's on the run in Pianvia or wherever.

Then he sees the red bus: *LONDON TRANSPORT.*
He's been in England all along. *What's real? What's
going on? Who can you trust?*

I'm asking myself those questions as the movie
ends and I fall asleep.

TWENTY

DECEMBER 29

At ten the next morning, the Cayenne pulls up behind the O'Toolemobile. AmberLea comes to the door. "Have they called? Have you got long underwear on? What happened to your face?"

My first answer to AmberLea is no, the second is yes, the third is "I'll tell you later." I'm as ready as I'll ever be for something I don't want to do. Skiing is the kind of thing Grandpa loved, not me. Any activity where some part of you is not touching the ground should be against the law. "I don't know about this," I say. I shrug on Bun's sport shell. It's too large. I take it off and pull on one of Deb's fleeces first. "Hat," says AmberLea. All I've got is my new one. "We're twins," she says.

"Triplets." I'm thinking of Toby. "Listen, I should stay in case they call."

"C'mon." She tugs my arm. "There's no use hanging around here worrying. If you've got your phone, they can call. Hey, you've done some tidying up!"

"It felt weird with the chairs upside down."

It's cloudy outside, not too cold. I thought we'd go north to ski, but we go east on the 401 to a place called Brimacombe. I keep checking to make sure my phone is turned on. AmberLea rides with me in the back. Toby and Tina are chattering up front. First I tell her how I got jumped last night. AmberLea looks worried and sympathetic. Good. I don't want too much sympathy, though, or I'll look wussy. "Anyway, I fought them off." I shrug. "Had to be SPCA." Looking out the window, I ask casually, "Do you, uh, hang out with Toby a lot?"

"Yeah. He's a sweetie. He brings, like, a different perspective to things. Did you know he and his brother sold some software to Apple for three million dollars when he was only fifteen?"

"No, I guess I missed that." When I was fifteen, I was figuring out *Donkey Kong*.

We get to Brimacombe in barely an hour. Ski equipment comes out of the bin on the roof rack. "I don't know about this," I say again as AmberLea walks me to the equipment rentals to get stuff for me.

"It's going to be fun," she says. "Their website said rentals come with a free lesson. Or I can give you one. Which do you want?"

I want to go home, practice my Michael Caine accent, start a romance with AmberLea and later have Bun walk in, saying, "Guess I better call Roz, huh?" Those things aren't on the table though. "Was Toby on the Olympic ski team?" I ask sourly.

"What? No. His dad was. In '94, I think."

"Maybe I could have a hot chocolate in the chalet."

"*Spencer.*"

Whatever I was going to say next is drowned out by a car that badly needs a muffler job.

We rent stuff for me. I feel like Frankenstein in the boots, especially after I snap into the ski bindings. A slender guy with a blue jacket, aviator shades and a big black mustache poles up shakily. He looks as if he's trying to make up his mind about lessons too. "Lesson from you," I say to AmberLea.

We go to the Baby Bunny hill. AmberLea shows me how to sidestep up the gentle slope. From the top, Baby Bunny seems to have morphed into Mount Everest. "This," says AmberLea, "is how you snowplow."

The snowplow actually turns out to be okay. I get down and up the hill a couple of times. I only fall over when I get distracted by AmberLea in her ski stuff, which includes a short yellow jacket and red skinny jeans. I'm a huge fan of skinny jeans on AmberLea— on many girls, in fact—but these red ones make a great combo with my blue ones. It's another reason we're perfect for each other and, like I said, the only reason I fall seven times. Really. Anyway, I take her picture on my phone. She videos me skiing. We watch it. Let's just say I'm not a natural. She shows me what to do differently. I try again, just missing a crash with the black-mustache guy, who has fallen over at the bottom of Baby Bunny. It's nice to know other people can't ski either. "Better," says AmberLea. "Now, point your skis in the same direction." Uh-oh.

After an hour or so, I graduate to the Bunny hill. There, I get to ride the Magic Carpet to the top instead of sidestepping. I'm moving up in the world, literally. AmberLea leaves me to take some runs on the bigger hills. She waves from the lift. I wave back and almost fall off the Magic Carpet. Hands steady me from behind. It's black-mustache guy.

"Thanks." I push my glasses back up my nose.

"No worries." He coughs, covering his mouth. He's wearing striped wool gloves I've seen before someplace. I stare, then have to turn away. It's hard enough riding the Magic Carpet without looking backward. At the top I hang back, pretending to fuss with my boots. Black Mustache starts down the hill. I follow. It's a slow trip. Black Mustache is even worse at skiing than I am. By the time we're down, I've noticed something interesting: a little bundle of blond hair poking out under the back of his pulled-down tuque. I've also done some thinking.

Toby's at the bottom. It's chalet time. AmberLea is already at a table; Tina is in the washroom. Black Mustache comes in and looks our way before sitting down. "That guy," I whisper. "I think that's Dusan, the SPCA guy from the streetcar, in disguise. I need you to decoy him while I check on something."

"What's the plan?" says Toby. We all look at each other. There's a pause, then AmberLea sighs. "I guess I'll have to take off my clothes."

TWENTY-ONE

AmberLea jumps up, grabs me by the hand and walks me to the exit, past where Black Mustache is sitting. She nuzzles my neck and whispers, "Follow my lead."

Outside, she pulls me past where the skis are stacked. Then she turns, throws her arms around me and kisses me. I'm so surprised, I almost inhale my glasses. Still, it's a great feeling—until I realize she's not really kissing me, she's whispering lip to lip. "Hug me back. Turn to the right so I can see. Okay, he's watching us. Keep hugging me and back me against the wall." I do my best. Her hands run across my back and up into my hair. We're against an equipment shed with an open garage door. "Now I pull you in here, and unless he's a real perv, he'll leave us alone for a bit while we trade clothes." She tugs me into the shed and past a snowmobile and unzips her jacket.

It's a good thing we're close to the same size. In fact, AmberLea is a little bigger than me. Her red jeans feel funny. "How do you wear these?" I ask.

"Shut up and dress. And no peeking."

I snap on the ski boots. My rentals are red; hers are white. Naturally, they're the only thing that's too small. I'll manage. I zip up AmberLea's jacket. We don't have to trade hats, but she tucks her hair up. "Glasses." She snaps her fingers. "I need your glasses." She jams them on, then swears under her breath. "How do you see in these bleeping things?" I don't bother to tell her they're not that strong. "I hope you know you're the only person in the world I'd do this for." She bumps into the snowmobile. "Now, stay in here until you see him follow me." She ducks her chin into my jacket collar and steps out of the shed. I wait one minute, then peek out. A blurry AmberLea has my rental skis on and is joining the line for the chairlift. Black Mustache, or Dusan or whoever he is, is doing his best to hurry after her.

I wait until they're both in the air, then step out
of the shed and Frankenstein-walk to the parking
lot. It takes a little longer without my glasses,
but I find the car, two rows over from the Cayenne:
an old gray Honda Civic with a sagging rear bumper.
I peer inside. By O'Toolemobile standards, it's neat as
a pin: a Starbucks Tall cup in the driver's-side holder,
an apple core on the gritty floor mats, a scraper for
the windshield, a box of tissues and what I think
is a parking ticket. I try the doors; they're locked.
I move to the back of the car. One end of the bumper
is attached to the car with a big version of one of
those notched plastic fasteners you sometimes
get with garbage bags. I try the hatch release and
get lucky. It's unlocked. I lift the hatch and fold
back the compartment cover. There's a container
of washer fluid, a set of jumper cables and a leather
messenger bag. I open the bag.

Inside, a tube of something labeled *Skinbind*
nestles in a bundle of yellow fur. I jump back,
thinking it's an animal, then gingerly pull out what
looks to be a fake beard and mustache. They're like
the stupid disguises I brought back from the cottage.
Below them is a file folder and a CD jewel case. The

jewel case holds an Aiden Tween CD. In the folder are snapshots of Deb, Jer, me and Bunny. One of Bun has been shot through a wire fence. I recognize a Creekside building in the background. There's another of Jer and Bun getting out of the van at O'Toole Central, probably the day Bun came home. There are also photos of AmberLea and Toby and me stepping out of the elevator in the lobby of Aiden Tween's hotel.

What's left in the bag is even creepier. It's a small cardboard box stamped with numbers and labeled *HOLLOW POINT*. Inside are two tidy rows of bullets, like miniature moon rockets. My times around guns have never been happy, and I know what "hollow point" means from the movies: the heads of the bullets flatten on impact to rip a bigger hole in whatever they've hit. I take the bullets out of the box and put them in AmberLea's jacket pocket. Next, I scrabble up some stones from the gravel of the parking lot and dump them in the box, so that it weighs about the same as it did before. Then I put everything back just the way I found it. Before I close the hatch, I take the jumper cables and use the jagged copper teeth on one of the clamps to tear the plastic strip holding the right side of the bumper to the car. The end of the bumper clonks to the ground. It should take a while to fix, maybe long enough for us to go home on our own.

TWENTY-TWO

We get back to the city around suppertime, well ahead of whoever's tailing us. When we'd met up again, Amberlea told me she'd taken the chair to the top of the highest run and made sure Black Mustache got off too before she started down. A while later, after we'd changed back into our own clothes and I'd discovered she'd split my jeans, we saw the ski patrol bringing down someone who could have been our guy. I almost felt sorry about the bumper. The bullets, I'd flushed down the toilet.

I did more thinking on the way home, and I know what I need to do. Thinking had been hard, too, because it seemed as if AmberLea was leaning a little closer to me than she needed to. I'd tried leaning her way, but the shoulder belt messed me up.

At the hotel, AmberLea gets the dairy calendar with the music in it from the front-desk safe. "Want me to go with you?" she asks.

"Nah, I can handle it," I say. Really, I do want her to come with me, but it would be wussy to say so.

"I think you're doing the right thing. Sorry about your jeans."

"No problem," I say, even though they were my favorites.

"Call me when you're done."

The duty officer at the police station doesn't bat an eye when I tell him I want to report a kidnapping. It's only when I start trying to explain the whole thing with Bunny and the SPCA and the movie, and I pull out the calendar, that he tells me to hold on. He makes a call, then gets another cop to take me upstairs to see someone else.

The second cop shows me into a room that has a table with a telephone, a couple of chairs and the classic mirror on the wall—two-way, I'm guessing, based on every cop movie I've ever seen. A video camera stares at me from a bracket near the ceiling. I unzip the shell and fleece, because I'm starting to get hot, and sit down, which at least hides the split in my pants. Then I do my best "innocent" act all over again. It's that kind of place.

The cop who comes in could be right out of a movie: big, with a bullet head and buzz-cut hair, tie loose, collar unbuttoned, five-o'clock shadow so dark that his gum-chomping chin is blue. Good, I think. Right now a take-charge pro is what I need. His eyes flick to the Muskoka Dairy calendar on the table, then back to me. "Let's take it from the top."

I'm barely started when the cop cuts in. "Bunny? That a nickname?"

I nod. "For Bernard. Bernard O'Toole."

He stops chewing. "Bernard O'Toole." He hammers at a laptop he's brought in. "Two Tecumseth Street?"

"That's it."

He rolls his eyes. "Not again. Your brother is a known affiliate of the Fifteenth Street Posse, a street gang in Mimico. He's also currently serving a year less a day in Creekside Juvenile Detention Centre. I put him there. So why don't you tell me how a punk in prison is being kidnapped at city hall? What kind of put-on is this?"

"It's not," I say. "He's out."

"He's *out*?"

"Well, just for Christmas, under this new CRAP program. You know: Constructive Rebound something something. His supervisor is Roz Inbow."

The cop swears a streak bluer than his chin and jabs at the laptop again. Then he looks at me. Now his smile reminds me of an alligator I met recently. I also know exactly why the guy looks familiar: he was at Bunny's court hearing. "Well, so he is," he says. "Supervisor Inbow. And I see there's a warrant out for his arrest for violating the terms of his release. So why don't you tell me where he is?"

"That's what I'm trying to do. I don't know where he is; he's been kidnapped."

"It runs in the family, huh? You're all smart guys? Quit covering for him before you get yourself in trouble too. He put you up to this? Where is he? With the Posse?" Saliva sprays. It wouldn't surprise me if a few teeth came out too.

"No, with the SPCA." He rolls his eyes. I feel sweat trickling under my arms. "Not the SPCA SPCA, but the Save Pianvia Counterrevolutionary Army SPCA. They've got guns, snipers. I found bullets this afternoon in a car at that Brimacombe ski place."

That gets his attention. "Ammunition? You found bullets?"

"Hollow point, the box said."

"Describe the car."

"An old gray Civic with a sagging back bumper."

"License?"

Oh. "Uh, I forgot to get it," I say. "But I got the bullets."

"Where are they?"

"Well, I flushed them down the toilet at the ski place."

"Naturally." The cop puts both football-sized hands flat on the table and leans toward me, leading with his Smurf-blue chin. "You know what the penalty is for making a false statement to police?"

"It's not false! They've grabbed Bunny because they want this!" I show him the calendar.

"I'll bet they do—1965 dairy calendars are really valuable."

"Not that. This!" I pull out the anthem.

"Uh-huh, and the flowers are by Picasso." He shoves back, hawks and spits on the floor. Suddenly a monster finger is right between my eyes. "Look, bleep-for-brains. Don't cover for your deadbeat brother. I should book you for misleading, but I won't. This time. Because instead, I'm gonna have the bleeping pleasure of watching you tell this load of horse bleep to the one who should really hear it."

You can fill in the bleeps yourself. He grabs the phone and punches in a number. "You're still here? Good. Come on down to number twenty-four... I know it's late...No, but I got someone named O'Toole here wants to see you. Yeah. Yeah, I thought you'd want to." He hangs up and gives me another alligator-Smurf smile. "There's still time to talk to the nice guy," he says. I keep my mouth shut, and we wait. The chair is hard. I can feel the split in my pants. I'm melting in my fleece. And all I can think is, Wrong again, Spencer.

The door opens and in buzzes a tiny Asian lady with short hair and glasses like mine except over-sized. She has a puffy overcoat on and a laptop case over one shoulder. She stops dead when she sees me.

"You're not Bernard." I know the voice. It's twice as big as she is, and it belongs to Roz Inbow. Even if she looks nothing like I'd imagined, and at least two centuries younger, I know I'm doomed.

Before I can say anything, Smurf Cop says, "Nah, this is a future client. His brother—or so he says. He's got such a horse-bleep story about your guy Bernard, I thought you should hear it before I toss him—or charge him."

I think of Harry, the *Ipcress File* guy, jabbing his hand with the wire as they torture him, and I feel an angry little surge. "It's not horse bleep," I say. "Bunny's been kidnapped and—"

"Whoa." Roz Inbow raises a hand. "I don't need to hear this. I don't want to hear this. It's already been a day."

"But my brother's been—"

"I said, whoa." Roz Inbow turns to Smurf Cop. The top of her head is level with his, and he's sitting down. And she's wearing boots with heels. "Harv, FYI, this is now filed orange anyway."

"*Whaaat?* It's not flagged."

"Just came down. Cut it loose. Now I'm out of here. I've got a headache." With that, she's out the door.

"*BLEEP*," says Smurf Cop/Harv. He glares at me and jerks his blue chin. "Out."

Outside, the cold air feels good, although maybe a little too cold at the tear in my pants. That's about all that feels good. Bun's in danger, and except for AmberLea and Toby, who may be busy having a romance, I'm on my own. I tuck the calendar inside my coat and look around for the gray Civic, just in case. All at once I feel very exposed.

"Mr. O'Toole!"

I register Roz Inbow's voice right away, but I don't exactly get called "mister" a lot, so it takes a second to realize she's calling *me*. She's waving from a car across the street. I wait for traffic to clear, then scoot over. The car's engine is running; the lights are on. "Listen," she says from the driver's seat. "Spencer, right? I just want to tell you officially that the warrant for your brother's arrest has been rescinded."

"Uh, great. Thanks," I say. "That's maybe not his biggest problem right now."

"I understand. I just wanted you to know. With an orange file, it's usually complicated. This is one less worry anyway."

"What's an orange file?" I ask. A gust from a passing car flaps the rip in my pants.

"I can't tell you. Sorry. But," Roz Inbow says, "I can tell you that I've had time to read Bernard's file. He's an unusual kid. There's more going on there than meets the eye. *So*"—she hesitates—"if I can do anything, unofficially, to help, I'd be willing to try. Here's my number." She passes me a business card like the one we already have at home.

"Thanks." This time I mean it. Because there is something she can do. If the SPCA knows about AmberLea and Toby, the music may not be safe with them. I check over my shoulder. "Listen, could you keep this safe till I need it? Like, tomorrow maybe?" I pull the calendar out from under the fleece. "There's a piece of paper inside. Don't show it to anyone. Don't even look at it."

Roz Inbow looks at me for a moment, then nods. She slips the calendar into her laptop bag on the passenger seat and zips the bag shut. "Don't tell me any more."

"Okay," I say. "I'll call you when I need it. Probably soon."

"I'm always around." She puts the car in gear and flicks the turn indicator on. "And, hey, don't let Harv get to you. All that bluster's just an act. He's a good guy."

"Right," I say. "How do you know?"

"I'm married to him," Roz Inbow says. Then she drives off.

TWENTY-THREE

I call AmberLea. She and her mom are going to the Christmas pantomime at the Royal Alexandra Theatre. Toby has begged off, so they have an extra ticket; do I want to come along? I pass. Skiing has left my muscles feeling as pounded as the keys on Harv's laptop. Plus there's that rip in my jeans.

"Where's the music?" she asks, whispering so her mom doesn't hear.

"It's safe," I say. "Not with me. I'll tell you all about it later."

"My phone will be on."

There's an awkward little pause, then we both say, "Later," and click off. I lurch to the streetcar stop like the Tin Man in *Wizard of Oz.*

At home, everything is the way it should be: no attackers waiting, no messages on the landline, nothing more out of place than usual. I have a shortbread from the cookie jar/gun holder. It tastes a little oily. Then I grab a hot shower, which feels so good I debate staying in it forever. Unfortunately, the hot water runs out, so I creak down to the kitchen to start some mac and cheese.

For the first time in two days I have a chance to wonder what my cousins have been doing since they raced off. I wonder who took the Walther PPK. DJ's too straight-arrow, and I know it's not Bun or me. That leaves Webb and Adam. It's a toss-up. Webb is the kind of guy, to tell you the truth, who's edgy enough that I wouldn't want him to have a gun. He might take it though. Adam and I talked about the new Bond movie, and he recognized the gun right off. I don't know why he'd want it though. That's a laugh. Why do *I* have a gun in the cookie jar? Why did Grandpa have them at the cottage? I pour a glass of milk.

By now the water is boiling. I stir in the macaroni and pour another glass of milk. I don't feel quite as stiff if I keep moving, so I start pacing a circle: kitchen, dining room, living room, hall, kitchen again. My thoughts circle, too, around Grandpa. I'm remembering the Wikipedia entry for Josef Josef, the dictator who talked to the Americans in the 1960s. What I'm thinking is this: if the United States was trying to cut a deal with Josef Josef, maybe part of his price was that they get rid of Zoltan Blum. Clint the killer might really have been a CIA guy, but he wasn't out to help Blum: he was tricking him. His real job was to kill him and get rid of the anthem. It's a scary thought: the person you trust to help you is the one who's out to get you. Kind of like *Ipcress*.

I stop pacing. It's time to eat. I finish making the mac and cheese and take the pot to the table. While I wait for it to cool a bit, I ask myself the next question: was the killer Clint actually David McLean? Did David McLean trick Zoltan Blum into hitting a golf-ball bomb? In one way, it doesn't matter—all that matters is that the SPCA thinks he did. In another way, it matters more than anything, because what I'm really asking is, could Grandpa D do this? And what for? Patriotism? Revenge? Justice? Money?

Part of me screams no. That's the part that can think up innocent reasons for why he had a piece of Zoltan Blum's music and remember that he imported Cuban golf balls. But I also remember talking about Grandpa and killing, in the kitchen before Christmas, and Bun blurting out something about ants. I didn't get it then, but now I do. One time up at the cottage, when Bun and I were in our bunks after lights out, he said Grandpa had showed him a bayonet or something with old dried blood on it from a good guy who had died. He told Bun he took it away from a bad guy. I asked what "took away" meant. Bun didn't know. All Grandpa had said was, *The good guys are the ones on your side.* After that, they'd zapped an ant nest with tins of Raid. Bun said Grandpa got right into it. I remember feeling jealous. I always figured Grandpa thought I was a wuss, because we never did much when it was just me and him, and killing ants sounded like fun. I reminded Bun that Jer said Grandpa was a *killer* because Grandpa flew bombers in the war. Bun had started chanting,

Grandpa's a killer, Grandpa's a killer, until someone called to him to shut up.

I wonder when the next call will come. I wonder where Bun is right now. I wonder if he knows who's on his side. I wonder if any of us do.

TWENTY-FOUR

DECEMBER 30

The call comes early. I'm awake instantly. Dusan's voice says, "You hef anthem."

I'm squeezing my phone hard enough to crack it. "It's in a safe place."

"Good. Many things happen. You hef been patient. There is change in plan."

"What? What do you mean? I give you the anthem, you let Bunny go."

"Soon. We did not know before of friendship with Aiden Tween."

"I'm not friends with Aiden Tween!"

"Do not pretend. You were seen. Media say his people look for how to make him more grow up. So. You will persuade him way to do this: sing our anthem at his concert on New Year's Eve."

"*What?*"

"We will know is going to happen when they call number I give and ask for translator for the words. We will give. He sings anthem, we release your brother."

"But I can't—"

"There was much argue about how sharp for blotzing ax. We decide to leave dull. Death longer, more painful that way. Here is number."

I grab a pen and scribble it down. The line goes dead.

For a long moment I stare at nothing, fighting down the panic that's rising with last night's mac and cheese. Then I'm in overdrive. I dig out the card Aiden Tween's manager guy, Sumo, gave me, and I start working the phones.

Sumo gets the first call. "Talk to me," is how he answers.

"It's Spencer O'Toole," I say. "You wanted the Pianvia movie from me."

"You got it?"

"Yeah, but I've got something even better about Pianvia, something no one else has, and it's perfect for AT."

"What is it?"

"I have to show you both. When can we meet?"

"One. Industrial Arts Studios. We're rehearsing on soundstage two."

AmberLea gets the second call. She sounds pretty groggy. "Stayed up late to watch *Alien* again." She yawns, and then her voice sharpens. "Did they call?"

"Yeah, and things have changed. I'll tell you later. Can you and Toby meet me to see Aiden Tween again at one? It's all set up. I'll explain when I see you."

"Well, I can. Toby's not here. He ditched the show last night and texted me that he'd see us later today."

"Where is he?"

"I'll tell you later. My mom's kind of ticked. She feels responsible, you know?" Then, "It's just Spencer, Mom," she says. I wait while she talks to her mom. AmberLea says to me, "I can pick you up. Mom's got friends meeting her here for lunch."

So far, so good. I'm starting to think I might handle this. The third call goes to Roz Inbow. Her oversized voice rockets out of the phone.

"It's Spencer O'Toole. I need to get the, uh, *papers* you have for me."

"Right. Just a sec," she says. Off the phone, I hear her blare, "For crying out loud, Sigmund, *of course* a gram of coke and a pit bull in a stolen car is going to be an issue for your parole. I don't care if they weren't yours. Go wait in the hall for a minute." Then come fumbling sounds and then she's blaring to me. "Spencer. There's, uh, a problem here. I took the wrong laptop case on my way out this morning. I've got Harv's."

"You mean—"

"He's got mine."

"Oh, no." The last thing I need is another hassle with Smurf Cop. I can imagine him at the station, finding the calendar and music and shredding them just to bug me. "Will he have looked?"

"No, no, it's okay. He'll still be at home, asleep. He's working four to midnight this week."

"I've *got* to have that stuff."

"I understand. Sorry about this." Her voice drops, almost unbelievably, to a murmur. "Trust me, I don't want anyone, including Harv, knowing I'm on an orange file, especially this one. Harv does seem to have a bit of a thing about your family. Look, when do you need this?"

I look at my watch. "Noon at the latest."

"Damn," Roz says. "I can't get there and back by then. Things are crazy this morning. Where do you live?" I tell her. "Okay," she says, "we're Parkdale too. I've got an idea. Have you got a friend who could help?"

We work it out. "I'll call him right now," Roz says. "Again, sorry about this. What name should I tell Harv?"

I only hesitate a second. "David McLean."

TWENTY-FIVE

I call AmberLea and ask if she can come half an hour earlier. Then I get busy. By the time AmberLea pulls up in the Cayenne, I'm as ready as I'll ever be. She's texting as I hustle out to the car, so she doesn't notice at first. I close the door and pull the scarf away from my face. "AAAGHH!" She bounces back in her seat. "What the—Spence?"

"Does it work okay?" I pat my new beard and mustache, partly to make sure they're still in place. "Do they look too fake? They cover up my scrape."

"What the—geez, no. They're good. I wouldn't have known you. Are those from your grandpa's cottage?"

"Yeah. The boots and hat are my dad's." I've got one of those blue Greek fisherman caps on too. It's a bit big.

"What's all this about?"

"I'll tell you as we go." I give AmberLea the address and she punches it into the GPS. Roz Inbow was right: her place isn't far away. We do a slow drive past, and AmberLea pulls around the corner. She stops but leaves the motor running.

"You don't have to do this," she says. "I could. I don't mind."

"I know," I say. I remember AmberLea decoying the cops at the rest stop last summer. And Dusan yesterday. "It's not that. I just feel like I have to do it." I take off my glasses and substitute a pair of Jer's aviator shades—the only style he'll wear. This pair is mirrored. "How's this?"

"Good," she says. She tucks some hair up under my hat. "Excellent. Go for it." Then she says, "I'll keep the engine running."

I give my beard-and-'stache combo one more pat, climb out of the Porsche and head back along the sidewalk. I'm stiff as a board from yesterday's skiing, and I'm not used to cowboy boots. Like the cap, they're a shade big. The heels make me feel as if I'm going to tip over. The fisherman cap sloshes around a little. I wish I had my glasses on, even if they are weak. *Go slow,* I tell myself. *Act confident. Bond.* I try to lean back, hands in the deep pockets of the curling sweater. There's a curling stone in my stomach. There's also a patch of ice on the front walk at Roz Inbow's. I skid but hang tough. Why aren't there treads on cowboy boots?

The house is a little bigger than ours and ten times tidier. My boots clomp on the wooden steps. I press the doorbell with a black-gloved finger. Deb's gloves. It's cold, but a drop of sweat slides from under my hat and nibbles the glue at the top of my beard. I manage to swipe it away and give the beard a quick pat before the door opens. I stuff my hands back in the sweater pockets. And now here's Harv the Smurf Cop, barefoot, in jeans and a gray Toronto Argonauts sweatshirt. This morning he seems even bigger, because the doorsill he's looming over is a few centimeters higher than the porch. His chin is even bluer. Harv does not seem to be the type who wakes up cheerful. He gives me the once-over. "Yeah?"

"David McLean," I say, giving him the mirrored aviators back. Only it comes out "Dive-id McLine."

I seem to have acquired a new accent. "Yew 'ave somfing fer me." I don't know where this is coming from, but I'll run with it.

Harv's hands are empty. He folds his arms across his chest and says, "I'll need some ID."

I don't move either. "Dowent be ridicooless."

"This how CSIS operates these days?"

"D'yew hev a list of stewpid questions, Harvey, or do they just come to yew?" What am I saying? I seem to have gone on some kind of Cockney kamikaze automatic pilot. Harv's blue chin juts out. His nostrils flare and his chest inflates. More sweat runs into my beard glue. I can feel it loosening. Harv stares at me. Before I get an instant shave or he can mush my ears into Jer's boots, I hear myself say, "Now stop muckin' abaowt and gemme that case. I've got bedder things to do than mess wit you, unnerstan?" I recognize the voice: I'm not a Bond, I'm channeling Harry Palmer in *The Ipcress File*. Why? Go figure. All I know is, it works: Harv goes purple above his blue chin. Then he snorts and steps back into the house. As soon as he does, I slap my drooping beard back into place. He's back with the laptop case. "Givvid 'ere." I hold out one black-gloved hand. "An turn aroun.'"

Harv snorts again and does his eye roll. He hands me the case and turns his back. I unzip the case, pull out the calendar, check for the music, then slide the papers inside the curling sweater, pinning them there with my arm. I zip the case shut. "Now, turn aroun', tike the case and go beck in the haowse. There's a good lad."

Harv turns around and jerks the case out of my hands. "Bleep you," he says.

"Tut, tut. You need to work on your bedside manner, old son. Almost a pleasure doin' bizness wiv you, Harvey. An' just to show there's no hard feelin's, you might wanna hev a look in the Baby Breeze Motel, las' unit. They've got an indoor garden there you'll love, and the handcuffs you lost. Just watch out for the alligator, heheheheh."

Harv slams the door. My mustache falls off.

I make it back to the car without skipping for joy or falling over. One would be tough with sore muscles and in cowboy boots, the other not so hard. "Your mustache is crooked," AmberLea says.

"Doesn't matter now. Let's get out of here." I peel it off, and we peel away.

TWENTY-SIX

We're barely a block away when the Bond ringtone sounds from my pocket. I dig out my phone. "Hello?"

"Hi, Spencer."

"Bunny?" I'd have fallen over if I hadn't been sitting in a Porsche. As it is, AmberLea swerves, then pulls over. "Bunny! Oh my god, you remembered my number. Where are you? Are you all right?"

"Jade gave me your number. I called her."

"You've been gone two days now, Bun. Are you okay?" I think about them arguing over how sharp the blotzing ax should be. "Can you talk?"

"That's what we're doing. I'm pretty hungry."

"Okay, good. Listen, Bun, where are you? We'll come and get you."

"I don't know exactly, Spencer. The mailbox on the house said *Newman*. I was in the basement. I could see out the window."

"Newman, okay. What can you see out the window?"

"Well, there's a fence, then the road and some stores in the distance. There's a guy talking on a phone, like us. And a speed-limit sign by the road. It says thirty."

"What else?"

"Um, up at the corner there's a muffler repair, there's a pizza place—"

"Wait," I say. Something starts to buzz inside me. "What kind of pizza place?"

"You know, it's got the blue sign with the white holes."

"*Domino's?*" AmberLea's hand is squeezing my arm. "Is there a Christmas wreath in the window?"

"I dunno. It's too far away. Then there's a wall and an alley."

"And the wall is covered with tags, right?" I'm practically shouting now.

"Yeah, and—"

"Just like the gym on Fifteenth Street!"

"Hey, that's right. I never thought of that." Buns sounds genuinely amazed. I remember the cheesy brainwashing scene in *Ipcress* again and Harry turning out to have been in London all along. Could it actually work like that? All I can do is play it slow and not confuse Bunny any more. Who knows what he's been through?

"Okay," I say. "I think I know this place, and it's closer than you think. Help me a little more, Bun. Is there a street number where you are?"

"I dunno, Spencer. Can't see any."

"Okay, Bun-man. We're on our way. Be careful."

"Spencer? What do these guys want from Grandpa?"

"It's about that spy stuff, Bun. They say it was Grandpa in the movie too. This guy named Dusan—"

"Susan?"

"No, *Dusan*. A guy with a beard. Maybe. He told me. It's complicated."

"Dusan has a beard. Him and Vi and Lubor kidnapped me. They put me in the car and took me away. They're the bad guys."

"That makes us the good guys, Bun. We're on our way. Stay cool."

"I will."

I punch off and turn to AmberLea. "AT will have to wait. We have to go to Fifteenth Street in Mimico." She lets go of my arm and punches it into the GPS. I punch Jade's number into my phone. *The good guys are the ones on your side.* We need a few more.

TWENTY-SEVEN

The Fifteenth Street Posse is run by a guy named Scratch. We kind of met last year. Scratch wasn't on my side then. Bun seems to think he was on his though. More to the point, he's here now.

Scratch is a dapper-looking guy, not much bigger than me, who dresses like he works in a bank but is planning to own it. I spot him through my fogged-up glasses as AmberLea and I walk into the Tim Hortons where Jade works. He's sitting at a table away from the windows with his back to the wall, wearing a fitted black overcoat and white silk scarf combo that Bond would go for. I shrug my Harry Palmer curling sweater higher.

Beside Scratch is a guy I'm guessing is one of the Posse. He's black, too, and in full hip-hop gear, from his giant NY fullback cap to unlaced Timberland boots.

"Buffalo Boy," Scratch says as we reach the table. "We meet again." He half stands and nods to AmberLea. "You were there too. That was a sweet bluff." AmberLea nods back. "This is X," Scratch goes on, nodding now at the other guy. "Ran with your man Bunny, who is our man too."

"X-*Ray*." The other guy winces. "I'm not some no-name X."

"That's true," says Scratch. "Now that you've told the world, let's take a walk."

"I'm not done my hot chocolate," says X-Ray.

"We'll get another later," Scratch says, buttoning his coat. "It'll taste better after some fresh air."

"Man, it's *cold* out there."

"Meter's running, X." Scratch slips a black tablet case under his arm.

"At least let me roll up the rim." X-Ray fumbles with the paper cup. We wait while he doesn't win anything.

We head out into the cold and walk the block back to Fifteenth Street. There's car traffic but not many people out walking. "Run it down for me again," says Scratch. AmberLea and I give him a recap about Bunny being snatched by the SPCA, Bunny's phone call and how what he sees from the window seems like Fifteenth Street. "We need your help to find him," AmberLea finishes. "We thought if he's in your territory, you'd know where he could be. Newman is the name on the mailbox."

"If it is Fifteenth, why wouldn't Bunny know it?" Scratch asks.

"They might have brainwashed him," I say. I know it sounds lame, but it's all I've got.

Scratch looks at me while he chews that one over. Finally he nods. "Okay. Uh-huh. It could fit. There's a house partway down Fifteenth we've been wondering about. Weird people moved in last month. White, with funny accents. Lots of coming and going, and they act strange. Don't know about the mailbox."

"Any of them drive an old Civic with a sagging rear bumper and a loud muffler?"

Scratch looks at me. "Dude, the whole neighborhood drives that car. You might recall that *I* drive one of those—though I'm upgrading shortly."

"Right," I say.

"Doesn't matter what their ride is. Today is the day we get acquainted."

We turn down Fifteenth Street by the muffler place. We pass the Domino's Pizza, the tagged brick wall of the gym. Up ahead, the speed-limit sign with a 30. "My god," says AmberLea, "it does all fit." My heart starts revving.

"All that's missing is a bus saying *London Transport*," I mutter.

"Huh?" AmberLea says. "Oh, like in *The Ipcress File*? I loved that bit."

I told you we were perfect for each other.

"Next block," says Scratch, his breath clouding the air. "Five houses in." I count down to a tired-looking frame house with smeary white siding. From here I can see a side window with a view up toward us. That could be the one Bunny looked out of. He could be looking out of it now. Scratch says, "You two turn down the next street. We'll take it from here."

"No way," I say. "Bunny's my brother. Besides, I might recognize someone."

"Right," says AmberLea.

Scratch sighs a little cloud. "They more likely recognize you."

"Not with this." I pull out the beard and mustache. AmberLea grabs the mustache and slaps it on herself. I stick on the beard and my shades.

Scratch just shakes his head. "Let's make it more difficult." He sighs. "Come on then."

A white SUV turns out of the side street ahead of us and rolls farther down the block, pulling in near the first low-rise apartment building. It has red-and-white government plates. Nobody gets out.

"Check it out," Scratch says.

X-Ray shakes his head. "New to me."

Then a police cruiser passes, like one did the last time I came here. X-Ray hunches into the collar of his down vest. Scratch just struts along. The cruiser passes the SUV and keeps going right to the end of the street, down by the lake, where it starts to turn around. It's just another day in Mimico, I guess. It doesn't feel like it to me.

Just before the cross street, Scratch says to X-Ray without looking at him, "Dress me up." He slows as he steps off the curb, just enough for X-Ray to jostle him. AmberLea nudges me. From a half-step behind, I see something slip from X-Ray's hand into the pocket of Scratch's cool black overcoat.

A gun. As we cross, Scratch says to X-Ray, "Who's around back?"

"T Bird and Ripple."

"Dressed?"

"Uh-huh."

"Good," Scratch says. To us he says, "Here's the rules. If you're really with this, I do the talking, you do the smiling and staying out of the way. If things, uh, *escalate*, bail. You don't want to have to go to emerg; they get nosy about puncture wounds."

"Got it." I swallow hard.

"Okay. *Together we fly*. Know that?"

"It's what Bunny's tattoo should have said. From Grandpa's squadron in World War Two."

"It's on my shoulder. That means, Bunny's in there, he flies with us, no matter what it takes. That's all there is to it."

We're almost there. Walking like this reminds me of the second-last scene in a '60s movie I watched in the fall, called *The Wild Bunch*. The old outlaws walk down the deserted Mexican street to the last shootout. Then the camera cuts to around the corner, where there's a whole army with machine guns waiting for them. The last scene, in slow motion, I'd rather not think about, especially in cowboy boots.

We go up the walkway and crowd onto the tiny concrete porch. On the siding by the door are two screws and an oblong patch of cleaner white where a mailbox would hang. My heart skips. There's a ratty blind hanging askew in the front window. Scratch takes a business card out of his tablet case, then knocks. We hear the tread of feet from inside. I draw in a quick breath. Then the door swings open.

TWENTY-EIGHT

"Welcome!" Standing in the doorway is a chunky, red-haired guy in his twenties. He's got a chin beard like the one I've slapped on and a smile wide enough to show off two acres of teeth so blindingly white that I'm glad I've got my shades on. His eyes are weirdly bright too. He's wearing an impossibly clean short-sleeved white shirt, tucked into black dress pants that are held up with a belt and suspenders. His right forearm has a big tattoo I can't quite make out. Pinned above his shirt pocket is a name badge: *Dwayne*.

Scratch nods and gives him the card. His hand goes back in his gun pocket. "Morning. City Planning and

Building Department. Just here for a quick inspection to make sure that the required repairs and upgrades were done as ordered. This is a rental, correct?"

"Shore is!" the guy says, "but CNI is hoping to buy when we take root here. C'mawn in." It's not what I'd call a Pianvian accent—unless Pianvia is really in someplace like Idaho.

Dwayne waves us in. We crowd into the little hallway. It smells of baking and fresh paint. In the little front room on the right I glimpse drop sheets, tins and a stepladder. I can see into a kitchen at the end of the hall. A dark-haired girl is at the counter, working away at something in a mixing bowl the way Jer does—except Jer doesn't wear a blue gingham dress with a white apron on top. Through the doorway on my left I see a man and woman in paint-spattered coveralls, putting down more drop sheets. "Welcome!" they call too. I give a little wave back.

"This won't take long," Scratch says, moving ahead. "Few things around the place we have to check for. Attic, basement, the usual. Wiring and plumbing refits mostly."

"Shore," Dwayne says again. "Hep yourself. Cellar's through the kitchen. We want everythang to be jes' right when we go doors open with CNI nex' week."

"CNI?" says Scratch.

"Church of Norman Intergalactic. This is our first missionary outreach in a foreign land. When our founder Norman Floog discovered the Book of Norman in the Walmart Dumpster in Boise, one of the first things the Throgs told him was that their mission was intergalactic, but we should start with international. Toronto seemed like a real good place to start." As he talks, I get a better look at his tattoo. It's a corncob with rocket tail fins at the bottom, blasting off. *Houston, we have a problem.*

It doesn't take long to go through the place. Ten minutes later we're back on Fifteenth Street. AmberLea has a *Book of Norman* bound in fake leather, Scratch has a DVD called *Alien, Not Alienated*, and X-Ray and I each have a stack of pamphlets and some cookies. The top pamphlet says *AlphaWays to the Lords.* Below is a graphic of the rocket corncob blasting off toward a stack of halos. "Thanks for trying," I say. "Bun would appreciate it."

Looking up from her *Book of Norman*, AmberLea says, "I just realized it couldn't have been there anyway.

The speed-limit sign is facing the wrong way for anyone to read it from the house."

I groan. She's right.

"Hey, you win some, you lose some," Scratch says. "We hear anything about Bunny, we'll let you know. Good luck. X, if I was you, I wouldn't eat those cookies."

TWENTY-NINE

We race across town to a part of the city called Leslieville. The big film-industry soundstages are down there. I got a tour of one in September with one of my classes. We park at Industrial Arts Studios between two white suvs. There must have been a special on this month. "Have you figured out what you're going to say?" AmberLea asks.

I groan. Aiden Tween is my only chance to save Bunny, and I've been too busy cursing the SPCA to think of what to say. "Well, I thought I'd…tell…uh, no."

"Leave it to me." She slams her door.

AT and Sumo are in a sleek Airstream trailer parked at one side of the giant soundstage. Other people are leaving, striding off into the dimness. On the practice stage, dancers are running a routine under the lights. A bass line thunders. The trailer door is still open. As we reach the steps, I hear Sumo say, "You're sure about this? It's not your—"

"Mah fans would freak if we cancel," AT says. "Remember Berlin? They'll have it covered. Besides, this is the right thing to do. It's mah risk."

"Our risk."

AmberLea shoves me up the steps. The talking stops. They're sitting in a mini-living room. Sumo is still in black. AT is in shimmery cargo pants, a sky-blue bomber jacket and a wooly blue-and-yellow hat with earflaps I've seen before, plus the gloves AmberLea gave him. Sumo gives us a Transylvanian Death Glare. "Talk to us."

AmberLea starts pitching. "So. You know Pianvia is trending. Get in now. They've banned music there, right? FREE THE MUSIC is your slogan, and we've got the way to do it: a world premiere for your concert tomorrow, a national anthem for a free Pianvia by its most famous composer. Written sixty years ago and never been heard. Banned, then lost, and now we've got the only copy. Sing it tomorrow night—new song, new year, new Pianvia. Get a film crew on it, and AT will own Pianvia, which I've got to tell you is hot in our age group right now. All you—"

"Perfect, we'll do it," says Sumo.

"What?" AmberLea is startled. I think she was just warming up.

"I said, we'll do it."

"Oh. Great!"

"Where's the music?"

I hand over the calendar. "Nice," says AT.

"Consider it yours," says AmberLea. She shows him the music.

From looking like you or me with two piercings and a five-hundred-dollar haircut under a stupid hat, Aiden Tween somehow sharpens into a different person as he scans the music. Quietly he begins singing, "Ba da be bum, dum dee doo, Ba da be bum boo…" Say what you want about his music, the guy can sing.

"AT has perfect pitch," says Sumo. "Sings and plays anything on sight."

Aiden Tween stops singing. "I like it. It sounds familiar already, you know? I'll want to take it up a tone." He sings a bit in a higher register, then says, "Let's do it. We'll definitely do it." He smiles for the first time.

"Really?" I feel myself go weak with relief. Bunny's going to make it.

"We'll get Jim to do an arrangement," says Sumo. "Those the words? How are we going to get them translated?"

"I've got a number right here." My fingers are trembling as I pull out my phone.

"No arrangement," says AT. "I'm gonna do it a capella. Just me, single white spot. Get me one a' their flags. Do their flags look good? That's a killer tune. We could have a hit with that tune. Man, I'd do it even if those—"

"Great, Aiden," says Sumo. "Okay," he says to AmberLea. "FREE THE MUSIC, but not free music. This is a business. What's your angle?"

AmberLea starts talking again. I stop listening and make my way out of the trailer. Bunny's going to make it.

THIRTY

Out on the stage, another song I don't know is pounding. The dancers are still bopping under glaring lights. You can see them from different angles on big screens above and behind the stage. Colors and camera angles change. Out in front of the stage, facing it from about fifteen meters away in the dimness, people cluster at a bank of glowing computer screens and tech boards that look as if they could run a space station. The tallest person looks familiar. It's Toby. I walk over.

"Spencer! Hey, how's it going?"

"Good. Things have changed, but I think Bunny's going to be okay."

"Fantastic." I'm so relieved about Bunny that when he raises his fist to do props, I match him.

I ask, "What are you doing here?"

"Oh, just hanging, you know. Turns out they're using the software already."

"Software?" I ask.

Toby sweeps back some perfect hair and says, "Just some stuff my older brother and I developed back when I was in junior high. Graphics stuff that interacts with sound and light effects. Highly effective for concerts. Apple bought us out, actually, before we could do much with it. I've just been making a couple of suggestions."

"Oh," I say, "right. AmberLea told me." I shrink back to normal in my cowboy boots. "Looks like AT has your hat," is all I can come up with to say.

Toby laughs. "Oh. Yeah. He has a way of latching on to things." In this light, Toby almost looks as if he's blushing. Somehow it lets me ask, "So like, you and AmberLea, are you, like, how long have you…?" That's as far as I get before someone jumps on his back. AmberLea.

"There you are!" she says.

Toby laughs and shrugs her off. Then he gives her a hug. "I called your mom, Hot Lips. She's cool. Told her I'd be along in about an hour. Just wrapping up here."

"Going good?" AmberLea gives him a private look. I'm thinking, *Hot Lips?*

"Going good."

I shrink a little more. Since the boots make me an inch taller, maybe no one will notice. Besides, a free Bunny is the main thing.

AmberLea and I head back out into the cold. It's bright after the shadows of the soundstage. "You should've stuck around." She nudges me. "They were so into it, I got us ten percent of the publishing on AT's arrangement of the anthem, plus a last visit to the cottage before they tear it down."

"Wow. Thanks for persuading them," I say. "How did you do that?"

"I dunno." She shrugs. "My father's in advertising." She pauses. "You know, I'm good, but that was almost *too* easy. Didn't you think?"

Now it's my turn to shrug. "Who cares? You saved Bunny."

Her chin has gone in. After a second she lifts it and squints a smile back at me. "Maybe our families are just meant to help each other," she says.

The SUVS are gone. As we get into the Cayenne, I clear my throat. "Uh, how come, um, TobycallsyouHotLips?" The last part spills out all in one word.

AmberLea blushes. The color goes great with her hair. "Ever seen *M*A*S*H*? The movie? Toby teases me that I look like the nurse character, Hot Lips Houlihan."

"Oh. I should check it out." Dumb, dumb, dumb. It's also a little late to say, "No, you're prettier," isn't it?

AmberLea starts the car. "That anthem is the real thing, right?"

"Hey," I say, "you found it."

"I know, but…did it sound familiar to you when AT hummed it?"

"Kind of." I reach for my seat belt. "Yeah, it did."

"To me too." AmberLea digs out her iPhone.

I laugh and say, "Maybe that proves it's authentic: Zoltan Blum's Wikipedia entry said he got accused of plagiarism on some of his songs."

"Maybe he should have on this one. Check this out." AmberLea plugs her phone into the suv's sound system and dials something up. Elvis Presley gushes out, *Love me tender…*

We stare at each other. It's the same song. AmberLea says, "So either AT was faking and can't really read music, or Zoltan Blum was a cheater. Guess which one I'm betting on?"

"Holy cow," I say. "The guy ripped off *Elvis*?"

"Obviously, he wasn't big in Pianvia. Anyway, I don't think Elvis wrote it either, but he sang it. Your grandpa played music, right? Do you think he knew?" She puts the suv in gear and we pull out.

I shrug. "I dunno. Why?"

"Well," says AmberLea, flicking the turn signal at the exit to the parking lot, "I was just thinking of—"

"Where we found it," I join in. Together we say, "Elvis belongs in the outhouse."

THIRTY-ONE

And now there's nothing to do but wait. We both realize we're starving, so we stop at an ancient-looking place called the Gale Snack Bar and chow down. AmberLea says she'll drive me home, but I tell her I'll just take the streetcar back from the hotel. We agree to go to a movie later at this cool old theater called the Revue, in the west end, not too far from where I live. They're showing a seventies movie Jer always talks about called *O Lucky Man!* Before that, all of us will go to some Parkdale restaurant her mom wants to try.

On the streetcar I try calling Deb. There's no point in trying to tell her what's really happened, because she won't believe me, but I can tell her I heard from Bun. She answers this time. "Spence! How's it going?"

"Okay, Mom. I heard from Bunny."

"See? I told you he'd call. Did you tell him to call me?"

"No, there wasn't time." In the background I can hear traffic noise and the chirping of a pedestrian-crossing signal. "Where are you anyway?" I ask. "I can hear cars."

"What? Oh, uh—Hamilton."

"*Hamilton?*" Hamilton is just down the highway.

"Hamilton, Bermuda, hon. It's a port of call on the cruise. Listen, did you get the number Bunny called from? Maybe I'll give him a ring."

"I don't think that's such a good idea, Mom."

"I'll weigh that in my deliberations, Spence."

"It's on my phone. Hang on a sec."

When I give Deb the number, she says, "Hmm. New York area code."

"Oh," I say. That explains a lot.

"Leave it with me, Spence. Just quit worrying and enjoy the show tomorrow."

"What?"

"I thought you told me you were going to see Aiden Tween tomorrow."

"Oh yeah." Did I tell her that? I can't remember.

"What's tonight?" Deb asks.

"Movie with AmberLea."

"Say hi for me. Be good. Use the debit card. Remember, Dad's home on the second, so try to have the place in only partial chaos. Love you."

As I let myself in at O'Toole Central, I get another call. Maybe it's Bun. It's Jade. "Hear you didn't find him."

"I even had the wrong country." I sigh. Jade tells me to keep her in the loop. I promise to. Then I pull off the cowboy boots, which by now are killing me, check the landline for messages and crash on the couch. It's dark when I wake to a pounding on the door, which turns out to be AmberLea. Her mom and Toby are in the car.

We go to a trendoid restaurant called Hopjoints. I know it's cool because all the servings are about the size of my big toe—and I have small feet. In a way this is okay, because there's zero on the menu I'd want to eat anyway. Toby orders sweetbreads, just to give you an idea. It doesn't matter; I'll get something at the movie.

I'm only telling you this part because something weird happens at the restaurant. I look around the room and who do I see at a table for two but Roz Inbow and Harv. I don't know whether they've seen me or not until Harv heads for the men's room. A moment later there's a tap on my shoulder. It's Roz. "How's it going?" she whisper-booms.

"Hard to say. Thanks for helping with the, uh, stuff."

"Sorry about the mix-up. From what Harv said, you have interesting friends. Said the guy was the real deal."

"*Really?* Oh. Yeah, well—"

"That's okay. Whoever he was, he gave Harv a good tip that paid off. We're out celebrating. Stay safe. Bernard too." As she leaves I think, I do have interesting friends, including Roz Inbow. It makes me feel a little better.

The movie is long and strange. It stars the actor from *Clockwork Orange*. He plays this guy who wants to be a success and tries all these different things, but he keeps getting tricked by people, all played by the same actors, who keep popping up in different roles, until…well, I won't tell the ending in case you ever see it. We all argue about it after, like you're supposed to do at film school. At least it's a break from stewing over Bunny. When we reach O'Toole Central, I crawl out of the Cayenne as Toby says something about "aggressive noncontinuity via the French New Wave" and AmberLea shouts, "No, the continuity is ironic picaresque." My contribution is swearing as I step into a slush puddle and soak my shoes. Before I fall asleep, I promise myself I'll look up what they were talking about tomorrow. The last thing I remember thinking is, the movie seemed like real life to me.

THIRTY-TWO

DECEMBER 31

I sleep late and wake up with a knot of worry in my stomach. AmberLea's mom invited me to go skiing with them again today, but I said no thanks. I wanted to be by our landline in case Bunny got a chance to sneak another phone call. He might forget my cell number, but he won't forget our home one.

I shower, telling myself that things are good—Bunny will be free soon. We've done everything the SPCA wants. They'll let Bunny go when Aiden Tween sings their anthem tonight. All I have to do is hang in. By the time Jer and Deb get home, Bunny will be back and due at Creekside. They can believe us if they want to. Maybe Deb will when she sees the mess in her office. Speaking of which, I can kill time before tonight's concert by getting O'Toole Central back in shape. I should text Jer, too, and tell him that the van won't start, so I can't meet him at the airport.

I make oatmeal for breakfast, with lots of brown sugar, and pour a big glass of orange juice. I'm Healthy Spencer, go-to guy, man with a plan. After breakfast I tidy the kitchen. Then I go upstairs, wipe the bathroom mirror and sink, stuff towels and dirty clothes in the laundry hamper and straighten up things the SPCA guys must have moved when they searched. By now I'm on a roll, so I go all out and take the hamper to the basement and put in a load of laundry. While it's churning I head back upstairs, haul out the vacuum and attack the living room. I plump pillows, pile magazines and clear away a fresh frosting of snack bags and drink tins. The place looks pretty good, but the worry still coils in my stomach like the vacuum cord at my feet. I tell myself there's no reason they wouldn't let Bunny go. Is there? We helped them. All that blotzing stuff was just a threat. They're freedom fighters: desperate, maybe, but not cold-blooded killers. They're supposed to be the good guys, for crying out loud.

I drag the vacuum into the hall and go at the stairs as if lives depended on it. The wall as you go up the stairs is filled with family pictures. It's the usual stuff, I guess. There are a few ancient people in old-fashioned clothes. There's Deb and Jer at their wedding, embarrassing baby shots of Bun and me. There are aunts, uncles and cousins, Grandpa Bernie and Granny Carol looking spry on Salt Spring Island, and in makeup doing their mime act on Haight Street in San Francisco in 1964. A two-year-old Jer sits in a stroller beside them, looking bored. Then there's a studio shot of Deb and her sisters as kids in matching dresses, and a snapshot of their mom, who died when they were young.

Beside these are two pictures of Grandpa David. One is black and white, from World War II. Grandpa and his crew are posing in front of their bomber, in flight gear, arms over each other's shoulders, grinning. Grandpa has a white scarf like Scratch's knotted at his throat. He's squinting a little, and a cigarette dangles at a smart-aleck angle from one side of his mouth. Above them, on the fuselage, is a stencil of a cartoon mosquito with a cigar and a machine gun, over the words *Together We Fly.*

The other is a color shot of Grandpa in his seventies, maybe. The only way you can tell is by how veiny and spotty his hands are. He's hefting a big fish by the gills, smiling under his floppy hat as he stands on the cottage dock. He's wearing his orange plaid shirt over shapeless tan pants and blue canvas deck shoes. There's a streak of fish blood or something across one pant leg. His clear gray eyes look right at you.

It hits me that both pictures are about killing. Are those the eyes of a killer? I feel myself frown. Dropping bombs in a war, catching fish and contract killing with exploding golf balls are not exactly the same. Anyway, the pictures aren't really about killing. You could just as easily say they're about good times: friends and sharing. Grandpa was always giving away fish he caught. I look back at the war picture. All those guys are barely older than me. Could I do that? I can't imagine myself there. Those guys must have been the best buddies in the world. Were some of them jerks? *The good guys are the ones on your side.* But what if you don't know for sure who's on your side? I remember the end of *The Ipcress File,* where Harry has to figure out which guy is the traitor who set him up, his gun swinging back and forth between two men. *You are a traitor,* said the note. Did it lie? Was it for real? Was Grandpa a hit man for the CIA? Was he a traitor? If good guys have to do bad things, does that make them bad guys? Does anyone ever think, Hey, my side is the bad guys?

I unplug the vacuum. The phone doesn't ring. When I finally leave for the concert, my shoes are still a salty, soggy mess. I pull on the cowboy boots again. Then I clomp to the cookie jar, take out the Colt .45 and slip it into my pocket.

THIRTY-THREE

The square at city hall is wall-to-wall people, or side-walk-to-sidewalk, I guess. Most of them are Tweeners with cold-looking parents. The decorations still flutter, but now the stage is up and lit, and music is pulsing from banks of giant speakers as one of the opening acts plays. Multiple video screens crosscut shots of the crowd with the band. The only morsel of space is the skating rink, where people still wobble and glide the way they did the night Bunny was snatched. Is it good luck or bad that the whole thing is finishing where it started? I'm as wired as any Tweener.

Tina has passed on the concert to have dinner with friends. We're supposed to meet her later. AmberLea, Toby and I make our way to the backstage check-in. The whole area is cordoned off with traffic barriers, cops and police tape. Our All Access badges are ready and waiting, and we glide through without all the screening. By now the security guys know us, especially Toby. This is good, because as we get to the check-in, it occurs to me that it might be hard to explain why I'm carrying an automatic pistol, especially when I don't quite know either.

Backstage is a canopied maze of RVs, equipment trailers, port-a-potties, you name it. Lights are strung. Bunched cables snake everywhere under protective rubber ridges. Impossibly hip and capable-looking people in headsets and AT hoodies bustle purposefully. Heaters standing near the canopy's ridge poles waft some warmth into the freezing night air. "That's Aiden's." Toby points to the biggest RV. "We won't bother him now. That one is for the band, that one the dancers. Hospitality's in that one." He points to an RV with tables, chairs and heaters outside its doors. People are clustered there, talking and chowing down.

To one side of Aiden Tween's RV stands a big circular tent, made of different colored strips of heavy material. "What's that?" AmberLea asks.

"It's a yurt," I answer, beating Toby to it for once. "Made of felt. From Tibet. My dad's in one right now. Not this one," I add.

"Aiden always has the musicians and dancers gather in there with him for a togetherness and focusing moment before the show," Toby says, topping me anyway. "Dope carpets inside. Handwoven, like the ones my uncle collects."

I liked it better when Toby was busy somewhere else. All I can say is, "Let's eat."

The hospitality spread has vegan, gluten-free, organic, local and also, fortunately, bad-for-you food. I grab a pizza slice and a hot chocolate, and we find seats by a heater. It feels good to sit; the cowboy boots are chafing again. As we eat, a blond woman walks by to another table, with a drink and something on a paper plate. She's wearing a tan knee-length parka and a purple-and-gold scarf. A leather messenger bag is slung over her shoulder. It's the woman I almost bumped into in the hotel lobby.

But now it all comes together: she's also a skier with a black mustache and a bearded blond hippie on the Queen streetcar. "Dusan," I breathe.

"What?" AmberLea's chin disappears.

"Over there. No, don't look! She might spot us." I tell them what I've just figured out. "She's SPCA, and she's here. What's going on?"

"She's the translator," Toby says. "I saw her yesterday. They called and she showed up after you'd left. She translated the words to the anthem from Pianvian to English and then Aiden invited her to the show tonight."

"She knows where Bunny is. I've got to find out."

"How?" says AmberLea.

"Maybe she's got something," I say. "Some clue. In that bag maybe. That's where I found the bullets, remember? We have to get it." My knees have started bouncing like crazy. AmberLea puts a hand on one to slow me down.

"Okay," says Toby. "Our advantage is she doesn't know we've figured her out. How do we separate her from the bag?"

"I'm on it," says AmberLea. She pulls out her cell phone and tells us what to do.

A minute later we all take off our coats as if we're settling in, and then I head back into the hospitality RV. From there I watch Toby and AmberLea chatter. AmberLea looks all around, then goes over to Dusan and, extending her phone, asks her to take their picture. Dusan smiles and stands up. Then AmberLea, a step or two at a time, gently leads them farther and farther away as she fusses over the perfect background, leaving Dusan's stuff behind.

I force myself to stroll, not run, to Dusan's chair, sit down and open the messenger bag as if it's mine. There's a cell phone, tissues, a balled-up pair of little black gloves, a hairbrush, lipstick. I look up. AmberLea has them over by the yurt, using it as a background and keeping Dusan facing away from me. I plunge back into the bag: subway tokens, coin purse, a slim wallet with twenty dollars, a bank card, driver's license for Jennifer Blum, 244 Berry Road, Toronto, Ontario, M8P 2J6. And a folded piece of paper. Out in the square, there's a roar as the openers finish. Instantly the backstage comes alive. For a moment AmberLea and the others are swallowed in the action. I open the paper.

PRESS RELEASE
JANUARY 1, 2013

The SPCA is shocked and appalled by the horrific murder of Aiden Tween as he bravely sang the anthem of free Pianvians everywhere, an anthem that the current brutal PPP regime has suppressed for fifty years.

There is no doubt the Pianvian government killed Aiden Tween. His savage assassination at his concert on New Year's Eve is yet another example of the cruelty and depravity of the PPP, who will stop at nothing to suppress free speech and human rights.

Aiden Tween was a longtime, dedicated supporter of the SPCA's struggle for a free Pianvia. He bravely gave musical voice to a people that have none. He became a martyr to our cause as he did so. We will forever be in his debt. Let him be an example to us all. Let the world rally to our cause with the same boldness. We extend our deepest sympathy to his family in this dark hour.

THIRTY-FOUR

I'm in my own chair when they come back. Dusan doesn't even give me a glance as she heads to her table. The messenger bag is where she left it.

"Did you do it?" AmberLea asks. "I stalled her as long as I could." Then, "Hey, what's the matter? You okay?"

All I can do is nod. My brain is working the way I skate: flailing around helplessly. I can't tell them the kind of horrible trap I've led everyone into, especially Aiden Tween.

Then Dusan is striding past us, cell phone in hand. I jump up. Toby looks at me questioningly.

I wave him off and follow her. I don't know what I'm going to do. She stops and starts, looking at her phone as if she's having trouble getting a signal. We're over near the yurt now. I step in front of her as she frowns over her phone.

"Dusan."

She starts a little, then looks up at me blankly. "Pardon?" It's the teachery voice I heard in the hotel lobby after we visited Aiden Tween that first time.

"Hi, Dusan. Nice to see you again."

"Sorry, that's not my name." She moves to step around me. I block her and say, "Oh, you have lots of names, just like you have lots of voices. And beards and mustaches—and a gray Civic with a busted bumper."

"I don't know what you're—"

"You're going to kill Aiden Tween."

For a moment she stares at me, as if she's trying to decide whether it's worth keeping on trying to fake me out. Then she jerks her head toward the open doorway of the yurt. We step inside. Like Toby said, the place is filled with fancy carpets. Lighting from somewhere gives it a soft glow.

Dusan turns to face me. "I'm not killing anyone," she says coolly. The fabric around us swallows her voice. "Aiden Tween will be lucky to die a martyr's death in the struggle against forces of oppression."

"I've read your press release for tomorrow."

"Then you know the Pianvian government, the PPP, is going to kill him."

"I know the SPCA is going to kill him and blame it on them."

Twin spots of red start to burn in her cheeks. "The SPCA fights for freedom. Sometimes freedom comes at a heavy cost. But not to you. All you have to do is stay out of the way, which is less than your grandfather did."

"My grandfather—"

"Your grandfather butchered my great-grandfather in cold blood," Dusan hisses.

"Zoltan Blum was your *great-grandfather*?"

"Of course." Her eyes glitter. I flash on her ID: Jennifer *Blum*. "And your grandfather blew him off the face of the earth with a bomb in a golf ball. There was nothing even to bury. And probably he said that somehow it was for the sake of freedom. Maybe he even believed it: it's easier to tell yourself that than 'I did it for the money.' Well, this *is* for the sake of freedom, freedom for a whole people, freedom your grandfather and his CIA masters set back fifty years. The whole world will rally to us if they think the Pianvian government killed Aiden Tween."

"My grandfather wouldn't do stuff like that," I say.

"He had the anthem." She shakes her head.

"There are a million reasons why he could have ended up with that song." I don't know what they are, but I keep babbling. "Somebody else could have killed your great-grandfather. You said he was scared and being followed. Maybe he gave it to my grandpa to keep safe and then got killed and *my* grandpa got scared and didn't know what to do with it, so he hid it. Ever think of that?"

"You think of this," she says. "Either Aiden Tween dies or your brother does."

"*Whaaat*? Why? The deal was, get Aiden Tween to sing the anthem. Period. I did that."

"But now you can make trouble for us, so the deal has changed. Deals often do. Ask your grandfather."

"He's dead."

"*Good.*" She spits at my feet. Something roils inside of me.

"I'll stop you," I say.

She smirks. "It's not me you have to stop. And it's far too late to stop anything."

"Oh yeah? Better check that box of bullets you carry around."

Now she laughs. "There is more than one box of bullets."

"I'm still going to stop you."

"Maybe you didn't hear me, little boy. Unless Aiden Tween dies, your brother will be killed. So you have a choice: him or your brother. A worthless pop star becomes an instant martyr for Pianvian freedom, which is better than he deserves, or your brother dies slowly and alone. I guarantee you, there will be nothing even to bury. Make a better choice than your grandfather did." Jennifer Blum walks out of the yurt.

THIRTY-FIVE

Bunny or Aiden Tween. I stand there staring at the riot of patterns in the carpets. They're a handwoven maze; there's no way out.

I have to save my brother. And that means someone else dies. How will they kill Aiden Tween? Snipers? A bomb? Screams, blood, chaos. To block it out, I try to imagine Bun right now. Is he handcuffed? Blindfolded? Staring at an ax? Does he understand what's going on? Has he made friends with them all? That would be a Bun thing to do. Maybe they've liked him too much to hurt him, or think he's just too weird. People react to Bun in odd ways.

As I cling to this thought, I'm interrupted by voices. People are crowding into the yurt: dancers, backup singers, musicians, then Aiden Tween and Sumo, surrounded by a moving mountain of bodyguards. Standing by the entrance I have a flash of hope: maybe they won't be able to kill Aiden Tween, with all this security. It won't be my fault if they try and fail. Will it?

They can all barely squeeze into the yurt. The security mountains back off. One of them stares at my clipped-on pass, then shoulders over and stands beside me. Everyone gets quiet. Aiden Tween looks tiny in his stage outfit. The gold of his hair exactly matches the sequins on his jacket. He looks pale at the edges of his makeup. He raises his gold-and-white gloved hands and starts to speak, his southern accent coming out stronger than I've heard it before. "Tonaght as we know, the show gon' be a l'il bit… diff'rent, and I'm countin' on y'all to make it a good one. If things, uh, get a l'il crazy out there, a few thangs not in the playbook, jes' stay cool an' know we're well looked after, here an' above. Everythang gon' be fine. All right, c'mon an' join hands for prayer."

I slip out of the yurt. I can't watch Aiden Tween saying his last prayer. I've sentenced him to death.

Now I'm a killer too. AmberLea and Toby appear. I can't look at them. Behind us, everyone bursts from the yurt and streams up the backstage ramps, ready to go on. The intro music begins to pound. "You want to watch the show?" AmberLea asks gently. I shake my head. "Let's go sit down," she says. "You go," she says to Toby.

We go back to the chairs and tables as Tween's show kicks in. His last one. I put my head in my hands and keep it there, for I don't know how long. Finally, AmberLea says, "It's going to be all right, Spence. Bunny will be all right. They'll let him go." She's trying to reassure me, but there's this note in her voice that tells me something I should have known all along. I look up.

"No, they won't," I say. "They'll kill him too." Friendly, oddball Bunny, who could look out a window and sneak to a telephone has seen and heard way too much to go free.

"Too? What do—?"

"Listen," I say, "there's not much time. Dusan changed the deal on me. They're going to kill Aiden Tween when he sings the anthem and blame it on the other guys. She said they'd kill Bunny if we tried anything." I swallow hard. "But she lied. They'll kill Bunny anyway. We've got to stop them."

AmberLea blanches. "Oh my god. We've got to tell someone. We've got to—where is she?" She looks around wildly.

"I don't know. But it won't be her. Remember she said a shooter watched the streetcar? I bet there's a sniper out front."

"Maybe we still have time. Come on!" AmberLea jumps up as Toby approaches. "When does he sing the anthem?"

"Soon," Toby says, "right after 'Ooooh, Ooooh Ooooh.' That's next."

"He can't sing it. Stop him! It's a setup. The SPCA will shoot him when he does."

"*What*?" It's the first time I've seen Toby lose his cool. "I've got to tell Sumo, get him offstage." He starts to run. "Call the cops!" comes over his shoulder. "I'll tell security."

AmberLea whips out her phone to call 9-1-1. There's no signal. "There were cops out at the barriers." She turns to run too.

"Forget it," I say. "The cops will never find the shooters now. They could be in the square, a building, anywhere."

Toby comes charging back as "Ooooh, Ooooh, Ooooh" kicks in. "He blew me off," he pants angrily. "Told me to shut up and that security is under control, that Aiden gets death threats all the time. He said there'd be a riot if we yanked Aiden offstage. What the hell's wrong with these people?"

The good guys are the ones on your side. "Okay," I say. "It's us against them. We've got to find her, make her call it off."

"How?" says AmberLea.

"I have a way."

"You two do that," Toby says. "I've got to protect him." He hurdles the steps into an RV. A second later he's out, sprinting past with a big purple-and-gold flag in his fist. "If they can't see him, they can't shoot him," he calls.

"Come on," says AmberLea. "Gotta find her. Split up. I'll take that side."

THIRTY-SIX

I jog up the closest backstage ramp, which is tricky in the cowboy boots. It's dim back here, and the glare from the lights out front is blinding. I push up my glasses and wait till my eyes adjust. Stacks of gear and equipment cases sharpen into focus amid the scaffolding. Shadows flit past in the gloom. None of them wear a tan coat or a purple-and-gold scarf. They're roadies and tech workers: Aiden Tween shows have a lot of special effects and stage and costume changes. I remember a clip I saw on TV where he's somehow beamed down to the stage from a spaceship or something. I look up. The spaceship sways on cables overhead.

I move forward. My guess is, she'll want to be as close as possible to watch Aiden Tween die. Out front, the lights change to cool blues and greens. I hear Aiden Tween oohing over the music. Back here, dancers huddle around a heater, their costumes barely reflecting the stage lights. A guitar tech stands at a rack of instruments, a little meter flashing red and green in the gloom as he plucks strings.

I slip past him, stumbling on a bundled snake of power cables, peering into the depths as I go. The stage lights shift, oranges and blues now. Ahead, they silhouette a stubby figure that would be Sumo, then a blocky, medium-sized one standing in the arms-folded-hip-cocked pose Deb goes for when she's going to disagree with something you say, then another mountain range of security guys. I pause by some kind of hydraulic thing that begins to rise as the song ends. A roar washes in from the crowd.

The light switches to a dazzling white that gleams off the top of Sumo's head. The other silhouettes all reach up and tug down the bills of their caps. I'm guessing the blocky silhouette is a woman, but she's too stocky for Dusan. A "hockey girl," as Jer calls Deb. Beyond them, I glimpse the stage. Aiden Tween is out there, all alone in the lights, in a sequined red matador jacket. The transmitter for his headset microphone pokes out beneath it, from where it's clipped to the back of his electric-blue leather pants. He raises a gloved hand.

Time is running out. I change tactics. I scuttle forward, as close to the stage as I can get, and duck into the gloom behind a riser. Staying in the shadows, I turn to face backstage. Glare from the stage lights might pick out Dusan's face if she's close enough. Behind me, Aiden Tween's speaking voice floats out over the crowd, his accent flattened out again.

"My life is about music, and sharing it with you." Another wave of cheering rolls in. "But there are places in the world where people can't hear music, not just my music, but any music. One of those places is called Pianvia. People are fighting for freedom there, the freedom to listen to music and to do other things too."

There's a stab of motion to my left. Two security mountains spring to life and tackle someone in a flurry of very large arms and legs. A second later they're strong-arming Toby and the flag past where I'm hiding. "You don't understand," Toby is pleading. "They're going to…"

I let them go. There's no time to wonder where AmberLea has got to; it's down to Dusan and me. I scan shapes and faces, shadows and glare. The lights shift. And there she is, way over to my right, by a bank of speakers and behind a chest-high equipment box, biting her lip, cell phone to her ear, waiting for Aiden Tween to die. Instantly, I'm running, stumbling through the dimness in a broad arc to come in behind her.

Onstage Aiden Tween says, "Tonight I have the honor of singing the national anthem of those brave folks, a song that has never been heard before. We're streaming it around the world to show we're standing up with them."

I lose Dusan for a second as I push through some dancers. I'm willing time to stop, running to beat the gunfire, the screams and pandemonium of Aiden Tween going down in front of thousands of people. I swing around a forklift and there she is, maybe fifteen meters ahead. Her coat and the messenger bag are beside her.

"Ladies and gentlemen, the national anthem of Pianvia Free."

In the second of silence that follows, I watch her jab angrily at her cell phone, then smash it down. Aiden Tween starts to sing.

Love you tender, love you true,
Pianvia, I will
Pungent pasture, splotnik too
And pigs have much to swill

I start toward her. She bends, pulls something from her coat. A gun.

Pianvia, Pianvia, fleever, blotz and yill
Oh my country, I love you and I mostly will
Springtime blizzard, summer rain, landslides in
*   the fall...*

She doesn't see me coming. She steadies her arms on the equipment box, taking aim. I'm six meters away. There's no time for anything but this. I pull the Colt out of my sweater, flick off the safety and swing it level with both hands. Grandpa. Bunny. Me. Maybe it runs in families. "JENNIFER," I yell.

She looks back at me.

I pull the trigger.

Click. Nothing. *Click.*

Too late, I remember I never checked to see if the Colt was loaded. I throw the gun at her and miss. It bashes the equipment box and falls to the ground. Jennifer Blum swings to face me, levels her gun and everything goes into slow, silent motion. I watch the knuckle on her trigger finger start to whiten.

And that's when AmberLea tackles her at the knees. The gun goes off. Something crashes above me, there's a yell, and they're down, wrestling. The gun hand gets free, clubbing wildly at AmberLea. I dive on them too, grabbing at that arm, pushing it to the ground. Everyone is writhing. I feel my glasses come off. The gun fires again. A knee rams into my stomach. I gasp, and my grip loosens.

From out of nowhere a foot in a scuffed Blundstone boot slams down on the gun hand. There's a nasty cracking noise, then a yell, and the hand goes limp. I look up. My mom is pointing a Glock pistol at Jennifer Blum's head. "Make my day," she says. She hasn't even seen the movie.

THIRTY-SEVEN

It's noisy in Aiden Tween's RV. Everyone is talking at once. I can't stop staring at the Canadian Security and Intelligence Service ID clipped to Deb's Kevlar vest and the holstered Glock at the waist of her jeans. Not to mention the earpiece. She's just finished telling us that they started monitoring the SPCA early in the fall and have been on the case ever since I first called her. "The problem was, we hadn't ID'd all of them and they kept moving around, switching phones. We intercepted enough to figure out they'd try to shoot Aiden Tween if he sang the anthem. That was going to be the only way to draw them out. So we spoke with him and his people and asked him to go along with it to help save Bunny, with us guaranteeing his safety. I've got to give him credit. He stepped right up, said it wasn't the first death threat he'd had."

"I thought that pitch I made was too easy," AmberLea says, nodding.

"Then we nabbed the shooters when they arrived at the concert and jammed the cell-phone frequencies so Jennifer Blum and the SPCA cell holding Bunny wouldn't know."

"Nabbed all but one," I say.

Deb nods and raises a hushing finger. She hasn't told AT's people how close Jennifer Blum came to killing him. "We should have taken her then too. We knew she was the brains at this end, but not part of the muscle. Anyway, we owe you big-time for being on to her. Thank you. It was also very brave and very stupid of you to go up against her unarmed."

"I didn't think I was unarmed," I said. "I had this." I hold up the Colt .45. "I found it at the cottage. In *The Anatomy of Melancholy*."

"Ah." Deb sighs. "Right. I knew I'd left something there. The bullets were in another book, *Yesterday's Spy*."

"Unfortunately."

"Fortunately," Deb says. "There are too many guns already. I'll take it." She holds out her hand. I'd picked up the Colt after the wrestling match; now I hand it to her.

"Where do you keep your gun?" I ask.

"An armory at Department of National Defence. I have to apply to sign one out. Anyway," Deb says, "the FBI and Homeland Security in the States have been staking out the Newman house where Bunny's being held, and judging by the amount of pizza their fake delivery guy has taken to the door, Bun is fine. They'll be going in any minute," she says, looking at her watch, "and they've assured me it will be a quick, easy takedown. I should get back to M3C to monitor."

"M3C?" AmberLea says.

"Mobile Communication and Command Centre," Deb says, as I realize Bond is warbling in my pocket. I pull out my phone. Deb says, "Looks as if we've stopped jamming those band frequencies." I squeeze through the crowd and out the RV door.

"Hello?"

"Spencer?"

"Bunny? Bunny! Where are you?"

There's a dead spot in the reception, then I hear, "—o. I'm in a car."

If he's in New York State, I bet that "o" is the end of Buffalo. "Fantastic, Bun! Rolling home." I'm actually jumping up and down. Bun starts to talk, but I can't stop. "Mom said you'd be okay. Man, am I ever glad."

"Mom?" he says.

"Yeah, she knows all about you. And guess what? She's CSIS."

A passing roadie looks at me curiously. I realize now I'm spinning around in little circles. I slow down and straighten my glasses. There's a crackle on the line, and I hear Bun say something: "…the cops. Tell…" Then he doesn't say anything, or there's another dead spot. I hear "getaway…skates…" and then "don't…"

"Don't?" I say back.

"Whatever—" I lose the signal again. "Can't hear you, Bun." Not that it matters right now. He's on his way home; that's what counts.

"Don't worry about me." His voice comes through loud and clear.

"Okay, see you soon. Have fun." I click off and hustle back inside. "That was Bun," I crow. "He's safe. On his way."

"Thank God," Deb says. She closes her eyes, puts her hand over her Kevlared heart and whooshes out a big breath. She hugs us both. After a moment she says to AmberLea, "Luckily, the rest here were amateurs. We had the other shooters rounded up the second they stepped off the streetcar."

"The streetcar?"

"Well, one took the subway, actually. We're talking low budget here, hon."

"Hey," I ask. "How did you get back from a cruise ship?"

"American Airlines, from our first port of call. Economy," Deb adds drily, "on my credit card. We're low-budget too. This operation maxed out department expenses for the next six months." She turns back to AmberLea.

"You could've told us all this," I complain.

"No, we couldn't, Spence. We couldn't risk you or anyone tipping them off accidentally. We made it an orange file—national security—so no one would meddle."

"So who is Jennifer Blum?" AmberLea says.

"She's a grade-three teacher with a sideline in voice-over work for commercials and cartoons. And she's Zoltan Blum's great-granddaughter."

The anthem is lying on a table beside us. I pick it up. "Did you know?" I ask.

Mom shakes her head. "Not a clue. Also just a coincidence that my working group has the current Pianvia file. I'd never known your grandpa might have been involved. I still don't recognize the picture in the movie."

I hand Deb the anthem. "It's evidence now," she says, pulling a ziplock bag from her pocket. "It never did much for the smell anyway." She smiles. "I've got to check in with M3C, talk to Bunny."

I follow her down the steps. "Hey, Mom, um, how long have you…?"

"They recruited me in grad school. Grandpa's suggestion. It can run in families." She gives me a tired smile. "And I rarely do this kind of thing. Usually, I'm more oversight and analysis. That's all I can say, really."

I ask the big question. "Do you think Grandpa did what they said?"

Deb sighs. She puts her hands on my shoulders and looks me in the eye. "I don't know, Spence. Maybe that's a sad comment in itself. Grandpa had many lives; we knew that. There's a lot we'll never know about. Maybe we shouldn't. At the end of the day, the David McLean I love is the one I knew and remember." She draws me into a hug. "And I can tell you, he would have been *so* proud of you tonight, just like me."

Outside the traffic barrier, a white cube van is idling little clouds of exhaust into the New Year's air. *CCTV SEWERSCOPE INSPECTION SERVICE* it says on the side. Deb walks toward it. "I'll try to get home tonight—or this morning," she calls, "unless I go to meet Bun. How's the house looking?"

I lie a little. "Super. Except for your office. The cookies are kind of oily though. And the van died."

As she walks off, I find myself wanting to ask her something else. If Bun was getting so much pizza, how come the first thing he said to me yesterday was that he was hungry? I don't ask. I've heard from Bun. Maybe there are things we shouldn't know, even at the end.

THIRTY-EIGHT

I go back inside. My glasses fog over, but I find AmberLea anyway. She's near Aiden Tween, who's standing with Toby in a circle of people. "Hot damn," AT is drawling, his accent back, "he'd a' taken a bullet for me!"

It occurs to me that Aiden Tween took a big risk to help save Bunny, and Toby took a big risk to try to save AT. Maybe I've been a little wrong about them. In fact, apart from Dusan/Jennifer, I've been wrong about a lot of people in the last few days. "He didn't know mah jacket was bulletproof and national security was all over it," AT cries. "He was willin' to lay it on the line!" His arm is draped over Toby's shoulder. Given the height differential, that's not as easy as it sounds. Toby's arm is over AT's shoulders too. They give each other a squeeze that's, um, well…let's just say maybe I've been wrong about other stuff too. "Hey," I say to AmberLea, "is Toby…?"

"You'd have to ask him," she says. "Let's just say he's a big fan."

"Wow," I say. "I sure had some things wrong."

"Like what?"

"Never mind. Do you want to go back to the hotel for the after-party?"

"Not really. Do you? I should text my mom. We're supposed to meet her soon, remember?"

"Okay. Let's leave the party to Toby."

She leads the way. As we squeeze through the crowd, I notice we're holding hands. I try to be cool about it. I think about the sexy bit in *Ipcress File* where someone asks, "Do you always wear your glasses?" Unfortunately, I'm the one wearing glasses, so I can't ask it. AmberLea saves me with a better line. Outside, she checks her phone. "It's after midnight. Happy New Year." She turns to me. We're still holding hands.

"Happy New Year," I say back. "What do you want to do?"

"Right this minute?"

"Yeah."

"Make my day," she says.

Which cues our kiss.

THIRTY-NINE

JANUARY 1

Deb still isn't home when AmberLea arrives at noon. This gives me time for a last tidy-up, which includes dumping the shortbread and washing the smell of gun oil out of the cookie jar. Jer calls, in from yurting with Grandpa Bernie. I say Happy New Year, tell him about the van and save the rest for later. I wonder how much he knows about Deb's other career. Deb texts to say there are things to wrap up, but she hopes she and Bun will join AmberLea, Toby and me for New Year's dinner tonight. AmberLea is going home tomorrow.

AmberLea and I drive north, same route as last time. At Gravenhurst we detour to go by the cottage AmberLea's grandma owned. The place is shuttered, the road unplowed. A real-estate sign with a red SOLD sticker on it is nailed to a tree. We sit in the Cayenne, talking and holding hands for a few minutes, and then I navigate us through Bala and on to Port Carling.

At Grandpa's cottage, a fresh snowfall has wiped our last visit away. I see the neighbors have gone home too. Stray flakes drift down as I climb out of the SUV. "You want to do this by yourself," AmberLea says. It's not a question.

I stomp through the snow. It's drifted around the back door, but I clear it away and let myself in. The gray light and stillness are like being underwater. Every sound is magnified. I open the secret compartment and take out the golf balls.

Down at the shore of the frozen lake is silence. The same wind that drifted snow around the back of the cottage has scoured the ice clear. The sky is white. With numb fingers, I scoop a ball out of the net bag. I hold it for a moment, gathering my strength.

Then I heave the ball as high and as hard as I can, out over the ice on the lake. For an instant it vanishes into the purity overhead. Then it begins to fall.

ACKNOWLEDGMENTS

As Eric Walters likes to say, *he who goes fastest, goes alone; those who go farthest, go together.* Stories and books are seldom purely solitary creations, and this one was no exception. I think we traveled a long way.

Many people deserve credit for the good bits; anything you didn't like should come straight back to me. First off, my thanks again to Eric Walters for the initial series idea and for generously inviting me to take part. I've had a fantastic time with this. Also, my thanks to Richard Scrimger and John Wilson, who got together with me over a beer one night (imagine the three of us hovering over one bottle) as we came up with the themes of espionage and dubious loyalty that drive this second series. While he's still hovering, further thanks to Richard for his ingenuity and enthusiasm in again linking our stories. Hats off also to Norah, Shane and Sigmund for their willingness to share ideas and companionship on the road as we promoted the first series and got this one up and running.

As always, my thanks on the home front to Margaret and Will for their patience, good humor and advice as they listened, read, reread, hand-held and gently suggested things far too sensible for me to ever think of on my own. Sometimes I think I only write so I can listen to their input.

Then there's the Sanders family (to whom I owe a gramophone and ski tips), Muskoka expert Frank Rolfe, Ed Greenwood, who can conjure a DVD of *The Ipcress File* and Bond trivia with equal aplomb, and the nameless owner of the crocogator/grow op establishment reported in the *Toronto Star*. You can't make up stuff like that.

Coda is intended to be an affectionate spoof of classic espionage tales. A number of writers and titles are name-checked in the story, particularly Len Deighton, whose words also provided part of the epigraph for this book. My thanks to all of them for countless hours of reading pleasure.

And I can't wait a moment longer to thank Sarah Harvey, my editor. Her keen eye and ear, humor and willingness to thrash out a plot point or character gave me confidence that it would all work out in the end. Kudos and a medal for perseverance (and bravery) to Sarah as well for editing all of the Seven titles, and to the folks at Orca who work so hard on the series.

Finally, I'd like to thank you, the reader, not only for hanging in all the way through a long set of acknowledgments, but for supporting Seven. You make all the difference.

TED STAUNTON divides his time between writing and a busy schedule as a speaker, workshop leader, storyteller and musical performer for children and adults. Ted is the author of numerous books for young readers of all ages, including *Puddleman*, the Morgan series and the acclaimed *Hope Springs a Leak*, which was shortlisted for both a Silver Birch and a Hackmatack Award. His most recent novel is the YA mystery thriller *Who I'm Not*. Ted lives in Port Hope, Ontario. *Coda* is the sequel to *Jump Cut*, Ted's novel in Seven (the series).

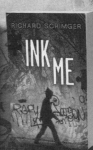